STAR CROSSED

J.E. Taylor

AN OTHALA WITCH NOVEL

Star Crossed © November 2016 J.E. Taylor

An Othala Witch Novel

For additional information contact:
www.JETaylor75.com

Edited by Midnight Library book Services

Cover Art: Rebecca Frank, Bewitching Book Covers, LLC
(bewitchingbookcovers.com)

ABOUT OTHALA

Many years ago, the Original Sixteen witches were able to contain an outbreak of demon-like creatures from overtaking the earth. But doing so came at a cost. For the human race to survive, the world had to be divided into sixteen sectors, trapping the ravagers to the outer lands beyond, and trapping the humans in.

The Original Sixteen served as regents over each of these sectors, and when they died, the strongest of witches took their place, using their own personal enchantment abilities to protect their sector. In the process, communication was lost. The only solace that remains is the knowledge that if another sector fails, their own may still survive.

But what happens when your sector is the one to fail? What happens when the world inside your walls is just as bad as the one outside them? In this collection of sixteen dystopian paranormal romance tales, each and every one of the sixteen sectors is about to find out.

View the entire collection at

www.fallensourcery.com

Star Crossed

**No matter which side of the coin she's on,
Star is destined to lose everything she loves.**

To keep Sector Eleven in his bloodline, Jaden has to marry a pure witch. Born into the Regency, his challenge is to find a wife who satisfies his mother's criteria while also managing to love him. Easier said than done when ambition supersedes the connection of hearts in a love mandate.

When Jaden asks Star to help him find a suitable mate, she agrees, but her heart doesn't want any part of it. Forced to serve the Regency since she was born, Star has been raised to hide her magical ability from Jaden and his mother, for fear the Regent would carry out her promise to destroy Star if she ever showed a propensity for magic.

Star is not sure which is worse, exposing her secrets to the man she loves which will have her exiled to the ravagers, and certain death, or playing matchmaker and losing Jaden to someone else. No matter which side of the coin she's on, she's destined to lose everything she cares about.

Chapter 1

The cold metal and concrete beneath us allowed a clear viewing of the constellations surrounded by the arc of northern lights. I shivered as the wind whipped through the broken structures, howling like a mad spirit. In the center of the city, this building remained, stretching towards the heavens, and if I reached my hand out, I swear I could almost touch the sky.

"You really think there's anything out there?" Jaden asked, interrupting my study of the vastness of the cosmos.

"I have no idea." I blew on my gloved hands, glancing at his strong profile before I sat up. "We should be heading back. Your mother would have a fit if she knew we climbed up here."

Jaden laughed with such a rich bass tone that it echoed over the decayed cityscape and stirred a warmth in the center of my being. Even through the thick coat, his muscles contoured against the dark fabric as his hands tucked under the back of his head. His bright green gaze moved from the star scape above us to mine.

"My mother would have a conniption, especially since she thinks I'm interviewing suitable mates." He rolled his eyes and his lips toyed with a smile, but he didn't budge from his stretched out position.

Just the mention of his obligations snuffed the heat right out of my bones. Jaden Mallory, the son of Regent High Witch, Samantha Mallory, had to get married before he turned twenty-five in order for the Regent torch to pass within his family, as it had over the last century.

His mate had to be of pure witch lineage, and not one of the hybrids most were these days. And his mate couldn't be just anyone. Those indebted in servitude were not allowed for consideration, which left me off the list of anything approaching an appropriate suitor.

Not that Jaden had a clue how I felt about him, never mind his lack of knowledge of the breadth of my powers, which I'd hidden all my life.

I think if he knew, he wouldn't be caught dead on this dilapidated building with me.

"She's going to blame me," I whispered.

"Chill, Star. I won't let her. I'll tell her the truth. That I dragged you up here just to get away from looking at one dingy profile after another. I couldn't deal with it anymore, and I needed inspiration."

It was my turn to roll my eyes. "Inspiration? Don't you mean some sick adrenaline rush?"

His dimples deepened. "Scared of a ravager attack?" he teased and poked me in the side.

I squealed and swatted him. "Jaden!"

"Star," he said, mimicking my exasperation.

I narrowed my eyes at him and sighed. "You know the magic is not as strong as it once was, right?"

"It will hold." He sat up, and we both looked to the west, to the edge of our sector where the protection of the invisible wall ended. From this side, there was no consequence in crossing through the barrier. But once on the other side, there was no way back. If the ravagers didn't get you, the electrified wall would.

Every now and again when the wind shifted, I caught the shimmer of the barrier. It was much closer to the buildings than I remembered from the last time we played hideaway from the adults.

I glanced at Jaden. "Are you sure?"

His gaze was locked where mine had been, and the small crease between his eyes deepened. When he climbed to his feet and offered me his gloved hand, I took it.

"I'm sure," he said, but he certainly didn't sound all that convincing. He glanced back at the barrier and sighed. "Sometimes I think I'd have a better chance out there than finding a wife my mother approves of within these walls."

His hand still gripped mine, and the slow rub of his thumb across the back of my knuckles gave my heart a start. I pulled out of his grip, feigning disinterest in his plight.

"Yeah, like getting married is so much worse than facing a pack of ravagers." I headed towards the crumbling stairwell and our safety lines.

"It is, especially if I don't love her," he mumbled behind me. "And all the ones my mother deems suitable are only stepping up because they want the position. It has nothing to do with me."

I glanced over my shoulder at him. "Are you sure about that?"

He sent a hard stare in my direction. "They are the worst type of vultures." He didn't wait, just clipped onto the rope and dropped the four stories to the beginning of the stable stairwell, bypassing the crumbling mass.

I clipped onto my rope and zipped just as quickly, giving him my more sardonic smile and a challenge in my raised eyebrow. I was probably the only woman in this entire sector that could match him pace-for-pace on an agility course without using magic.

Before he could unclip, I was off and bounding down the stairs at a speed that made my heart slam in my chest. Jaden's footsteps were only a fraction behind me, and his breath huffed in time with mine. I let out a laugh and chanced a glance over my shoulder.

His amused gaze met mine, and the race was on. Instead of bounding down the rest of the steps, I planted my ass on the rail and slid down the flight of stairs, jumping onto the landing and bolting towards the next one before Jaden could reach the same spot. Our laughter echoed against the concrete walls.

"That's not fair!" Jaden huffed as he came into view on the ground floor.

"Nothing in life is fair," I said and turned to continue the race, but my foot caught one of the fallen beams and I tripped.

The ground raced towards my wide eyes, and while I moved my hands to try to catch myself, I refrained from using magic to stop the fall. Twenty-two years of warnings from my mother were enough to stop me from easily halting my progress. If I revealed the extent of the powers infused in my blood, Samantha Mallory would have me fed to the ravagers out of spite.

It was no secret that the Regent barely tolerated my existence, especially since she blamed me for my father's refusal of her advances. She became obsessed with my dad after Jaden's father died, but he had no interest in the Regent or anything she had to offer. He loved my mother with every fiber of his being. His rejection had nothing to do with my mother being pregnant. It had everything to do with what a bitch the Regent really was.

With Samantha's fury sparked by scorn, my mother's magic was no match for the High Regent, and while it protected me, it could not protect my father from her wrath. Samantha Mallory exiled my father for exhibiting magical tendencies and cursed my mother into eternal servitude to the house of Mallory. She even went as far as threatening to exile me if I ever exhibited any magical abilities.

Every day of my life, my mother warned me of the consequences of displaying my talents. She taught me how to hide in plain sight, and how to fake the tests so I would appear normal.

So, I let the ground rush towards me even though I knew the impact was going to hurt like a bitch.

Jaden's soft command to stop halted my fall. I stared at the ground less than a half inch from collision and recovered enough to get my hands in place to stop a potential broken nose. His magic disappeared as fast as it came, and gravity pushed down on me, allowing me to catch myself before impact.

I pushed onto my knees and stared at him as he stumbled back and caught the stair rail to steady himself. Jaden had never shown the potential for magic. Samantha Mallory had made her stance clear to the kingdom when my father was exiled. Male witches were an abomination. A stain worse than a slave witch, and they had to be eradicated at all costs.

I didn't think he'd meant to let his secret out of the bag.

I wiped the gravel off my hands and knees. "Does your mother know?"

Jaden glanced out what remained of the glass doors and then back at me, and for the first time in our lives, I realized he was keeping secrets, too. The slow shake of his head along with the fear in his eyes relayed his discomfort. He wiped the back of his hand across his nose, and it came away bloody.

"After what happened with your father and every other male witch that ever showed their talents? Are you kidding?" He took a seat on the step and pinched the bridge of his nose, leaning forward. Bright red drops dripped, splattering in small circles on the concrete.

His mother's damnation of male witches had not stopped with my father, and this would clearly endanger her reign. He may be her firstborn son, but that wouldn't matter if this got out. She would exile him just like she had recently done to her own nephew.

He pulled out a pack of tissues to stop the flow, and after a moment, he glanced up at me, still holding the tissues to his bloody nose. The pallor of his skin whitened, and he took a couple long slow breaths before he wiped the last of the blood away and stood.

"You okay?" I asked and he nodded.

"That's a side effect of...whatever," he said and offered me an awkward smile.

"What kind of magic was that?" I crossed my arms. He didn't use the typical spell that I'd seen his mother use, or any potions to control my descent. He just uttered a single word, and my fall stopped.

He shrugged and shoved his hands in his pockets. "It's not anything like my mother's. I don't have control over the spirits or the elements," he said and finally met my gaze. "I don't need potions or spells to control things." He bit his lip, pleading with me silently.

I wasn't sure how to take his confession, and I certainly wasn't going to disclose mine. Not with the eternal warnings from my mother ringing in my ears. When he looked down at the ground, I glanced away, pondering his words.

"It's been years since I've done anything like that," he muttered, looking more like a little kid than a twenty-four-year-old man.

I gave him credit for stopping with just that explanation. I was sure he wanted to add not to tell his mother, or my mother, either, but he didn't. He never asked me to keep secrets, but I always did.

"You could have won the race," I said, offering my own crooked smile, changing the subject.

"You would have smashed that cute nose of yours if I hadn't intervened," he said, and his cheeks turned a brighter shade of pink.

I blinked in shock. I knew he cared about me, like one cared about a best friend, or even a little sister, but this was the first time he mentioned me and cute in the same sentence. It took me a couple of seconds to recover.

"You mean you could have stopped me from breaking my arm a few years ago?"

"No. I didn't see you fall. I have to see it happening to stop it, but I'm sure if I had been there, you wouldn't have ended up in a cast. I probably would have ended up outside the wall, though." He let out a sarcastic chuckle. "As I said, I haven't done this in years."

His honesty caught me off guard, and I had a moment to wonder before I blurted, "When was the last time?"

"When you were younger and ran out in the road to get the ball I threw to you." He shoved his hands farther into his pockets. I had a feeling if they weren't hidden in the confines of his jeans, they would have been shaking.

I remembered that day vividly. I had indeed run after the ball he threw and had looked up in time to see a bumper bearing down on me. "The day that car nearly hit me?"

The vehicle swerved at the last moment, avoiding a hit that would have sent me on to my next life. The driver swore he had no idea how he missed me, especially since he didn't remember turning the wheel himself. Jaden had passed out on the lawn that day, and when he came to, he'd had a bloody nose.

I stared at him and he nodded. The fact he saved my life sunk in deep, right next to my thumping heart.

"Why did you risk it for a lowly servant girl like me?" I asked.

He shrugged and scanned the empty streets outside. "We should head home," he finally said. "My mother is probably on the war path already since I blew off the half dozen interviews she set up."

My eyebrows rose. Jaden's love-hate relationship with his mother wasn't a mystery to me, but his more than blatant disobedience was. This was a new dynamic. He usually complied with her commands.

"What's wrong?"

"You mean besides being forced to get married to a power-hungry bitch who will tow my mother's line?" he snapped.

My jaw slowly dropped, and my eyes widened. It wasn't Jaden who would get the Regent seat; it was whoever he married. A witch was the only one who could keep the wall holding the ravagers in place, and his mother had made damn sure that in sector eleven, only a woman could be a witch.

Jaden would be as much of a slave to his wife's whims as we were to his mother's.

"If I can't find someone who loves me, then I'm sunk."

I understood that layer of fear radiating from him. A woman following Samantha's rules would have Jaden exiled the moment he made the mistake of displaying his powers.

Yet, Jaden didn't know what I was capable of.

I had command over much more than just the spirit world and the elements. I could read the ancient writings in the spell books his mother had hidden away from the public's eye. I understood the power held in those spells, as well as the consequences of damning another soul. I could make sure his potential wife was pure of heart and loved him as much as I did, and Jaden would never know.

He deserved true love and happiness, even if it wasn't with me.

Jaden and I walked back in silence. When we reached the gates, he hesitated and looked up at the heavens.

"Star?" he asked, his voice no more than a whisper.

"Yes?"

"I've never asked for your silence before," he started, and his gaze dropped to mine.

"You don't need to ask. It's a given," I said.

His tense features relaxed. He reached out and pulled me into a hug, catching me off guard.

"I can always count on you," he whispered against my ear. The heat from his breath sent a shiver through my blood.

When he pulled away, disappointment slithered through me. I rather liked his arms around me. Even though the hug was delivered as a friend, it still felt like home in his arms.

"And don't worry. I won't let my mother blame you for our road trip."

"Thank you." But I knew no matter what he said, his mother would blame me, and I would be given some horrid task as punishment. I just hoped it was on the outskirts of the palace so I could gather what I needed to protect Jaden from marrying an evil, power-hungry witch.

12

Chapter 2

"What were you doing running around in the iron city with that little tramp?" Samantha Mallory bellowed at Jaden.

"First of all, Star is not a tramp, and second, I dragged her with me because I couldn't stand the thought of interviewing your picks for a wife. I want to make the choice, not have you shove it down my throat!"

I hid in the hall, eavesdropping, with the aggravation of the Regent's words swirling in my stomach.

"You have no sense of how important a legacy witch is," the Regent snapped. "Besides, you are not the best judge of what is important to this sector. After all, look who you choose to fill your time with. A plain servant girl."

"At least she gives a damn about me, which is more than I can say for you." Jaden's footsteps resounded on the floorboards, coming closer to my perch beyond the cracked door.

"Jaden, do you know what is at stake?"

"Your precious legacy," he said in a mocking and bitter tone that accompanied an eye roll.

I didn't ever remember him being this derogatory with his mother. Of course, I didn't eavesdrop very often, either.

"I will choose a suitable wife," the Regent announced. "And you will abide by my decision."

"I would rather offer myself to the ravagers," he growled and I winced.

"That can be arranged," his mother hissed back.

His footsteps resumed, coming closer, and I quickly looked for a hiding place.

"Send that spying misfit in when you leave," she snarled.

He halted. "No. Star is not to be punished for my behavior."

I caught a glimpse of him in the mirror across from me in the hallway. He was close enough to see my reflection as well. The hardness in his features was as foreign as his tone with his mother, and I didn't know if his glare was aimed at me or not. I gulped the sudden lump in my throat, and it burned all the way to my stomach. The last thing I wanted to do was alienate Jaden. I slid out of hearing range.

He stepped out in the hall a few minutes later, and his gaze landed on me. There was a clear warning in his eyes and the tight set of his jaw.

"She wants to see you," he said through clenched teeth.

"Are you mad at me?" I whispered and waved towards the now open door.

He inhaled enough air to puff out his chest and looked past me before blowing the stream out. "You shouldn't have been listening," he said, returning his gaze to me.

Shamed heat filled my cheeks, and if I could fold into myself and disappear, I would have. I gave him a meek nod and slid by him.

His hand on my arm stopped my progression. "Be careful," he said.

The concern in his eyes gave me pause. It was more like the Jaden I knew, and not the angry, bitter man fighting with his mother moments before.

I nodded and he released me, but now my stomach fluttered with a symphony of nerves. My life had always been in the hands of the Regent, and in a moment of rage, she could snuff me out on a whim. The moment I stepped into the room, I knew that fear was warranted.

Samantha Mallory was every bit as gorgeous as her son on first look. Her long flowing ebony hair matched his short locks, and her green eyes pierced through me with accusation. The tight set of her lips indicated trouble, and when she spoke, the words were clipped and nasty.

"What lies are you filling my son's head with?"

My mouth dropped open, and I stared at her. "I'm...I'm sorry, your regency. I have no idea what you are talking about."

She stalked over to where I stood and towered over me in that intimidating manner that made me want to shrink into the floor. Thankfully, my inner rebel held fast as an indignant burn churned in my belly. I swallowed what little spit I had and forced myself to meet her angry gaze.

"You are filling his head with fantasies of love," she snarled.

I couldn't help it. I burst out laughing, right in her face. "I did no such thing," I said, feeling stronger with the laugh in my throat.

Her eyes narrowed. "You will get that thought out of his head, you understand?"

"How?" The question slipped out of my mouth before I could stop it.

"I don't care how, and for a little incentive, if you don't get him to accept my choice, then you can watch your mother torn to pieces by the ravagers."

My eyelids fluttered as I stared into her sharp emerald eyes. This wasn't a bluff. It was an ultimatum and one I couldn't dismiss. I gave her a slight nod, accepting the directive even though I planned on making it impossible for the union to last beyond that first kiss at the altar.

"Now that we have an understanding, I need you to replace all the flowers in the mansion before the sun rises."

It was one of her favorite punishments because she knew it was nearly impossible for me to find fresh flowers at this hour, which gave her a chance to practice her sadistic spells on a human when I failed the task. I had survived those torture sessions for years, and I knew I'd have to endure one more because my night hours were not going to be spent finding flowers.

"As you wish, my Regent," I said and curtseyed before taking my leave.

Chapter 3

I walked the darkened streets mulling over ways I could do both my tasks successfully. I wondered how much the Regent would freak if I cut up her prized rose bushes, but that would more than likely get me killed.

I sighed and refocused on the royal gardens. What I needed was fairly easy to find. Apples, apricots, lemons, rosemary, and basil—all ingredients that I could buy at the market, and all ingredients used in cooking. However, I did not want a record of my purchase, because if the spell I had in mind worked, Samantha Mallory would be on the warpath.

Pillaging the royal greenhouse was a risk as well, but at least I had a cover. I could explain away my basket, especially if my supplies were hidden by fresh picked flowers. As luck would have it, tonight the garden patrol had just completed their rounds when I snuck by the office. The two guards were engrossed in an intense game of cards.

I went straight for the fruit trees, picking two apples, three apricots, and four lemons. The basil and rosemary were equally as easy to procure. I snuck to the adjoining greenhouse and clipped a dozen carnations, flowers I knew infuriated the Regent, and almost got out of the building without notice.

"Excuse me?" a deep voice called.

I froze in place. I took a deep breath and turned, meeting the guard's terse stare. "Please don't tell the Regent," I blubbered, turning to show the basket of carnations I had plucked. "I need to find fresh flowers for the mansion before daybreak, and this is the only place I know of," I added with an ounce of panic in my voice, praying the guard would take pity on me.

He crossed his arms, glaring at me.

"I could always go to the rose garden," I whispered.

His arms slowly dropped along with the glare. "Run along. I won't say a word. And my advice, stay away from the Regent's roses," he called after me as soon as I was through the door.

Now all I needed was salt from sea spray. That was a longer trek, so I stopped at home, hiding the fruit and herbs before grabbing a small, clean jar and heading to the shore with the basket in case, by some miracle, I found flowers budding in the middle of winter.

By the time I got back home, I had just enough time to store the sea salt away and grab the carnations before the sun broke the horizon. If I was able to function after being Regent Mallory's lab-rat today, I would brew my potion tonight.

Knowing my punishment awaited, I took my time on the crisp walk to the mansion. The only bright spot was the thought of seeing Jaden, even if it was in passing while he went off to interview his mother's list of suitors.

This day was going to suck. I closed my eyes and said a little prayer to the gods to protect me, because I had a sneaking suspicion this was going to be worse than any other punishment I'd endured. I opened the door, and my gaze landed on the bright floral arrangement donning the entry table. The flowers looked new and in even better shape than the ones lying in the basket I carried.

I blinked and turned my gaze to the top of the stairs. Jaden leaned on the railing with a sneaky smile on his lips. He sent me a wink and then disappeared down the hall. He must have found out that his mother tasked me with the fresh flower mandate, which was one of her famously unrealistic tasks she gave to those on her shit list.

Jaden just saved my ass from a serious beating.

With the carnations in hand, I strolled into the Regent's office with my inauspicious offering. Samantha Mallory looked up from her desk with a cross expression that only worsened when she saw the bouquet in my hand.

"What the hell are those?" she asked, nearly spitting the words out.

"They are special for you," I said with all the innocence I could muster.

The Regent pressed her lips into a slit and glared at me in such a way that I shifted, wondering if it was really prudent to poke the bear.

"You know I hate carnations!"

I let my face fall. "I thought you hated chrysanthemums." I feigned horror, and it looked like she bought it. For the most part, Samantha Mallory did not know I had any common sense or the level of intellect that Jaden saw. I'd played the innocent fool for years, which was why she abhorred my friendship with Jaden. "I'm so sorry, ma'am. I'll get these out of here right away." I turned to leave.

"This is who Jaden needs to choose," the Regent said, and I spun back.

She handed me a picture of a sprite little blonde with a thin aristocratic nose and sharp dark eyes that reminded me of a predator. I turned the photo over and read the woman's dossier. There was no way this little pixie would be Jaden's type. All her hobbies were sedentary and centered around magic and potions and spells. Chemist and bibliophile were not what Jaden was looking for. He needed someone who wasn't afraid of adventure.

I gave Samantha a strained smile, feeling a little lightheaded for a moment before I nodded. "I'll try," I said, handing back the picture.

"You will make sure this is the woman he chooses, or I will exile your mother."

I met her glare. "What is so special about this one?" I asked, trying to keep the snark out of my tone. I barely managed it.

Samantha cocked her head, studying me as if she picked up on my hesitation.

"She is suited for this position, and I will not let my son's romantic ideas get in the way of what sector eleven needs."

The venom and conviction in her voice sent a shiver down my spine. I gave her a nod and wandered out of the room. The daze I was in cleared as soon as I crossed the threshold, and I realized the Regent had tried to influence me with some sort of compliance spell.

I finally found Jaden in the study and closed the door behind me. His grumpy expression brightened at the sight of me.

I waggled my finger at him. "Do you have any idea what your mother would have done had she caught you filling the vases?"

His cockeyed grin surfaced. "I can only imagine what she would have done had they not been fresh."

He didn't know the half of it. My gait slowed, and I stopped in the middle of the room studying him. Did he know about the countless times I was her guinea pig? Had his attentions on me been as much a ruse as what I portrayed to his mother?

Jaden's smile faded, and he stood and closed the distance. "Star?" he asked with earnest concern.

I stared into him, trying to see any sort of manipulation on his part, but all that was there were his bright green eyes filled with worry.

Without concrete knowledge, I decided to test him.

"What happens when someone disappoints your mother?" I asked, feigning the same wide-eyed innocence I had in front of Samantha.

He huffed and turned, crossing until he dumped himself in the seat. When he waved at the monitor in front of him, he said, "This."

I joined him behind the screen, and it shuffled from one girl to the next.

"Hours upon hours of this crap," he mumbled. "Help me find someone, Star."

I snorted and he glanced up at me.

"I need you to pick for me. You are one of the best judges of character that I know. If you think one of these vultures could fall in love with me, I'll believe you."

I stared at the screen and let the picture of that girl shuffle through a couple times before I reached over his shoulder and stopped on her. I hated myself for it. This was as wrong as the spell I had tucked away in my arsenal, but it was the reality of our situation. I had to suck it up. Otherwise, my mother's fate would be the same as my father's, and mine wouldn't be far behind.

"That one might be worth the time to talk to," I muttered under my breath and stepped away before he saw the disgust painted in my soul.

Jaden leaned forward, reading the same details I had in his mother's office moments before. He wrinkled his nose and glanced back at me. "She seems a little too obsessed with magic."

I shrugged. "She's cute." It was all I could muster.

"Seriously?" He gawked at me. "She looks like a deranged fairy." He waved towards the screen.

"What's the harm in talking to her," I said, flustered at his unwillingness to take the bait.

He sighed. "I wish you were on the list," he said under his breath as he turned towards the computer. The squeak of his chair almost drowned out his words, but not quite.

I wasn't sure I heard him right anyway. I stood frozen, staring at his reflection in the monitor. His green eyes locked on my image, not the pixie on the computer.

He shut off the picture and the screen went dark, but he remained in place just staring at me. "You heard that, didn't you?"

I let out a strained laugh and he turned, facing me. With his piercing green eyes on me, I was stunned into silence, but I managed a one-shoulder shrug. Heat layered on my cheeks, and I forced myself to not flee the room. My heart had already decided to play a twelve piece concerto at the prospect of him feeling remotely the way I did about him.

He stood and stepped close enough for my brain to fog. "When I get married, will you still be my friend?" he asked softly.

His eyes were so intense I almost leaned forward to catch a kiss off his pouting lips, until his words sunk in and my heart plummeted.

"Of course," I said and swallowed the bitter tears lining my throat, willing them to stay hidden. I turned to leave, but his hand found my forearm.

"Star?"

I paused but couldn't look at him, not with the bitter swirl in my stomach.

His finger hooked my chin, forcing me to meet his gaze.

I tightened my jaw. "Can I do something else for you?" I asked, forcing my tone to stay on the chilly side.

He dropped his hand and shook his head, but there was something akin to hurt flooding his eyes.

I took leave, and instead of starting my daily chores like I usually did, I headed for my private quarters, knowing I would be paying for my insubordination dearly. But right now I didn't care.

Lemon drifted from under my pillow. I almost pitched the ingredients across the room, but logic rang through my devastation. I could deal with this matchmaking ruse knowing he saw me as just a friend, but today he'd slipped, much the same way he had with his magic last night. If he felt the same, I couldn't stand by and let him marry someone else.

Tears choked me, but the pillow muffled my sob.

Was it all a ploy to get me to reveal my secret? Or did he truly care?

And if he really cared, he had to know I would never agree to be his mistress.

The click of the door pulled me out of my thoughts and I turned, expecting my mother, but Jaden stood inside my room, his eyes wide at the sight of me crying.

I turned away, mortified. "Get out," I said into the pillow.

Instead, he had the nerve to take a seat next to me on my simple cot. His hand landed on my back, and I wanted to scream.

"Talk to me," he said in that impossibly soft voice that made me want to tell him all my secrets.

"Please go away."

"I can't. Not until..." He let the silence fill the room, but his hand gently trailed over my back in slow strokes that lit my imagination.

I finally looked up at him. "If your mother finds you here, she will kill me."

A small smile appeared with a huff. He glanced out the tiny window in my room. "She'd disown me," he said and looked down at me. "Which doesn't sound like such a bad idea at the moment."

I swiped my wet cheek with the back of my hand and sniffled. "What are you babbling about?" I asked, trying to adopt the tough girl persona. The one that hid my true feelings for all these years.

He raised his eyebrows.

"Well?" I said, turning away from him and sitting up, hugging my knees so I had some barrier between us.

"Come here," he whispered in that commanding tone.

I laughed. A crease appeared between his eyes, and suddenly I understood. Those soft commanding tones were in line with the same one he used yesterday to stop my fall.

His eyes narrowed. "How come you don't obey?"

"What? You think because I'm your servant girl, I just have to comply with your every whim? Fuck you, Jaden. Now get out!"

I pointed at the door, but he grabbed my wrist, yanking me into his arms. His lips were on mine before I could contest.

I struggled in his tight grip.

"Damn it, Star, just kiss me," he muttered against my lips.

The need dripping in his voice silenced my protest, so I stopped fighting him, allowing the kiss. My protection barrier crumbled under the intrusion, making my entire form tremble as his tongue mingled with mine.

I pulled away from the kiss, nearly jumping to the other side of the bed like I had been electrocuted. My hand flew to my mouth, and my heart slammed the walls of my chest.

Jaden ran his hands through his hair and folded over with his elbows resting on his knees. He looked like a man who had just lost everything.

"You have to go," I said, and he glanced at me, sitting up. "This is impossible, Jaden." I pointed between us.

He opened his mouth and then closed it, glancing at his hands before his gaze returned to mine. His eyes pleaded in the same way they did last night when he asked me not to say a thing about his powers.

"What is it that you see here?" I asked, responding to his silent plea in a way that I detested. The fact I would do anything the man asked rubbed me wrong on so many levels.

His small laugh, coupled with a sigh, gripped my heart. "I've always seen a future with you."

He reached for my hand, and I let him take it. We both stared at the connection. The electricity flowing between us became a living, breathing being, one that demanded attention.

"I thought I had more time to change things," he said, meeting my gaze. "And until today..." He slipped his hand from mine, using it to comb his hair back in exasperation.

While I wanted to hear the rest of that sentence, I couldn't afford his sidetrack from what his mother wanted. My mom's life hung under the whim of that crazy witch.

"You need to do what your mother says." I despised the conviction in my voice, and my chest hurt from the immediate sense of loss.

"You want me to marry her pick to run this sector?" The surprise in his voice reflected in his wide-eyed stare.

My voice wouldn't cooperate with my brain. I could not force a yes over my lips, so I closed my eyes.

"Do you love me, Star?"

The soft question drew my breath in a hitch. I opened my eyes to his imploring green ones.

Not enough to sentence my mother to death. The thought leaped from the depths of my mind, but I never voiced the words. Neither did my heart's immediate yes preceding the thought.

"You're my best friend," I said when my wits regained balance.

His jaw tightened. "Tell me how you feel."

That commanding tone was back, followed by the crease between his eyes when I didn't speak.

"The only other person that doesn't work on is my mother," he mumbled, and his eyes narrowed.

"I thought you said you didn't use your powers," I countered, turning the tables on him to avoid his suspicious glare.

He blinked and recoiled a fraction as if I'd slapped him. He let out a nervous laugh and looked at the ceiling. "I might not have been totally honest about that."

I crossed my arms and cocked my head, waiting for an explanation.

"I've been able to influence people in the past, and they never seem to be the wiser. It's like my command becomes their idea," he said softly. "Influencing people's actions is easier for me to do than controlling matter. The only person that seems to be impenetrable to my influence is my mother." His gaze sharpened. "And you. Why is that?"

I stared at him and shrugged. My protection spell must have been just as strong as Samantha's, and that knowledge gave me a start.

"What exactly have you made people do?"

He bit his lip. "When I was in school, I would use it to make sure I got all A's."

My mouth dropped open.

"My mother's expectations were unreal," he said in his defense. "I only got a few B's over the years, but my mom expected A's. And she threatened a wealth of punishments if I didn't bring her the grades she wanted."

I could see Samantha issuing those kinds of ultimatums. Hell, she held my mother's life over my head to get me to comply. I wondered what Jaden would do if he knew the extent of his mother's cruelty.

He shook his head as if to clear it and then focused on me. "You keep dodging my question."

I offered him a tilt of my lips and a shrug. "I don't exactly have an answer for you."

He studied me and sighed, accepting my answer with a slow nod. "I am going to refuse to marry anyone my mother lines up for me."

Panic filled every pore, and I bit my lip to keep a plea from escaping. Instead, I said, "Do you really think that is wise?"

He closed the distance between us, threading his hand into my hair and pulling me to his lips. Just the feel of his mouth on mine pulled a trembling gasp from me. He took advantage of taking me by surprise. Before I knew it, he had me pushed back on the cot and his hand cupped my breast. The slow rub of his thumb over the fabric of my shirt sent tingles from my chest all the way to my fingers and toes. I let the bliss continue, deepening the kiss before I finally pushed him away.

"That's not a best friend kind of a kiss," he said, his eyes filled with the same desire sweeping through me.

"Yeah, well, unfortunately, that's all that we can ever be." Voicing the reality triggered a hole to blow through my chest. I swallowed the harsh pain and offered what I hoped was a smile.

Even if my protection spell worked, he'd eventually find the perfect wife. And it wouldn't be me.

Chapter 4

With all my ingredients except for the dried sea spray simmering in a pot on the stove, I skimmed the mixture, removing any remaining remnants of fruit. I took a deep breath and picked up the small satchel containing the sea spray to sprinkle it into the simmering potion as I cast the spell.

"I hunt by seed, flower, and fruit to ward off evil intentions at the root. I invoke thee, great goddess of day and night, protect Jaden with all your might. As this potion passes Jaden's lips, let it cast a curse on any mate who accepts his marriage vow without purity of love in her heart. Spirit of the fire, let the wheel of fortune spin, and if you find blackened intent, smite her at the first wedded kiss."

I pricked my finger and squeezed a drop of blood into the mixture before lighting the black and red candles on either side of the stove. I stirred nine more times.

"One, two, three—so mote it be."

A puff of smoke rolled from the pot, so I stopped stirring and turned off the flame to let the potion cool. My heart thundered in my chest, and I swallowed the fear that bloomed. If this didn't work, Jaden would be tied to a loveless marriage and hiding his true self for the rest of his life.

As someone who walked that path every day, I wouldn't wish it on my worst enemy. I filled a separate pot with ice and poured the concentrated potion into the pot, cooling it to a drinkable temperature.

With the liquid now cool, I poured it into a glass of shaved ice chips and poured myself a glass of plain lemonade. With both glasses in hand, I crossed the yard and entered the mansion through the servant's entrance. I found Jaden in the same room he had been in earlier, but instead of looking at the screen, his head was slumped back on the chair and his mouth hung open. His soft snore rumbled through the room.

I cleared my throat, and he twitched in the chair. His eyes flew open, blinking to focus on me.

He wiped his mouth with the back of his hand and gave me a sheepish smile.

"I thought you might be thirsty and figured you could be my guinea pig." I held the glass out to him. "I made a new fruit drink."

His eyes lit up, and he took the glass. I had a history of making some pretty awesome drinks. He tested it with a small sip then closed his eyes and took a second sip.

I nibbled my lip, waiting for him to drink it all up. When he smiled and opened his eyes, I let out a slow breath.

"This is really good," he said and then downed the rest of it. The green of his eyes shimmered as the spell settled inside him.

I sipped mine and smiled at him, feeling much less anxious about his future. At least now he wouldn't have to bow down to whoever he married.

Now that I knew he was safe, all the questions I had forbidden to enter my mind in my bedroom bubbled to the surface.

"Why now?" I asked when he handed me the glass.

A half-smile formed on his lips. "I slipped up twice in the last twenty-four hours."

"Are you sure it was a slip, or was it just a test to see my reaction? To see if I'd run to your mother and tell her what you've done," I said, my tone just as terse as the thought.

He straightened his back, stiffening at the question. His lips pressed together, and the anger that sparked in his eyes made me swallow.

"I've never played games with you." He reached out and grabbed my wrist. "But you've played plenty with me, haven't you?"

I stared at him and tried to yank my hand away. "What the hell are you talking about?" I snapped as the tray in my other hand teetered.

The glasses tumbled off and shattered on the ground, but Jaden still kept his grip on my wrist, ignoring the broken glass.

"You and my mother," he growled and pointed to the computer.

My heart thundered in my ears, and I glanced from the proof of my culpability back to him.

"Jaden..."

"Don't give me a line, Star." He let go and stepped back, putting his palm in front of me. "Tell me the fucking truth. There is no way in hell you would pick that girl out of the pool. And so help me god, if you lie, I will know."

My entire form shook as the truth tumbled out. "There are other lives at stake," I said, staring him down, suddenly more angry with him than I'd ever been. He'd put me in this impossible position where if I lied, I would lose him, and if I told the truth, I would lose him as well.

He recoiled. "Lives?"

I pressed my lips together.

His eyes widened. "She threatened your mother?"

Just the fact he pulled that out of thin air shocked my heart. The horror in his expression added to my misery. I didn't answer. I couldn't. If I confirmed it, the Regent would kill my mother.

"You have to marry that one," I squeaked out. "She's the only one who can keep the barrier in place," I added, knowing that wasn't exactly true. I had read the ancient spell books. I had memorized every spell, every potion that lay within those pages, but there was no way

Samantha Mallory would let me step into the Regent seat. I tried to swallow the lump in my throat.

He stepped close, glaring at me. "You're talking about the lives of the people in the sector?"

I nodded, because it was better than putting my mother in the firing line.

"Then what the hell was that in your room?" he asked, closing the distance between us.

I tried to back up, but he grabbed both arms and pulled me against him. My entire form trembled.

"Tell me, Star, what is it that you want?" His feral whisper tickled my ear.

The word 'you' played on my lips, but I clamped them closed and twisted out of his grip. My feet moved fast, and air singed my lungs the minute I cascaded down the mansion's front steps. By the time my wits took hold, I found myself standing on top of the same building Jaden and I had been playing on last night.

I dropped to my knees, relishing the cold burn of the wind on my face, stealing my breath and peeling the tears from my eyes. I glanced in the direction of the edge of the building, wondering if I ordered the elements to make me fly, if I could soar right over the danger of the wild and transplant myself somewhere where there wasn't a Regent, or Jaden, or any worry about the death of those I loved hanging over my head.

I let the chill penetrate every cell. I didn't want to feel. I wanted to be as cold as the Regent was. The sun dipped below the horizon and I shivered.

"I thought you never turned down a real challenge."

I stiffened. It figured he would know exactly where I'd go. I bent my head. "Leave me alone, Jaden," I said loud enough to be heard over the wind.

"I will if you answer one question." The gravel behind me crunched, and then his hands were on my shoulders.

His touch undid me, and the sob that had been caught in my chest escaped. Instead of asking the dreaded question, he pulled me onto his lap and wrapped his arms around me, holding me while I cried.

"I've known you all my life," he said, smoothing my hair. "And I have never seen you this distraught." He kissed my temple. "It's like your heart is breaking, and there isn't a thing I can do to fix it."

His soft words pulled another bout of tears from my shaking form.

He lifted my chin so I'd meet his gaze. "Do you love me?"

My breath hitched. "Do you?"

His palm cupped my cheek, wiping my tears with his thumb. "Do you think I'd come running after you if I didn't?"

It wasn't a direct answer, but the softness in his eyes shot straight to my heart. I wiped my nose on my sleeve and cuddled under his chin.

"How much of our friendship has been real?" he asked, still using his soft tone.

"All of it, despite my mother warning me to stay away," I said.

He stiffened, tilting my head up to look at him. "Your mother forbade you from being friends with me?"

"Can you blame her?" I said, sniffling again.

His gaze traveled to sector eleven's barrier. He gave me a slow nod. "I guess I can understand, considering."

"What about you? How much of this has been real for you?" I asked, since we were obviously doing some weird quid pro quo.

"All of it. I was warned, too, and even threatened at times." He offered me a shrug and an attempt at a conciliatory smile. "That was the motivation for getting all A's."

I huffed a laugh.

"You've been my motivation since you turned thirteen," he said and sighed. "When you finally bloomed, you blew my mind. One day you were this smart-ass kid, and the next you were this sexy goddess who had no idea what the hell she did to the guys around her."

"What in Samhain are you talking about?"

"You." His hand moved from my hip, up the curve of my side to the edge of my breast. Jaden's eyes flashed with such intensity that I almost scrambled from his lap, but his grip on me tightened. "You are beautiful," he whispered.

I rolled my eyes. My nose probably was all red and runny to match my eyes, and my hair was in knots from the wind. Beautiful didn't cover me right now, and even at my best, I had never looked in the mirror and saw what he was referring to.

"I have wanted to kiss you for years," he said, taking my face in his hands. His lips covered mine, catching me by surprise like he had earlier in my room.

I kissed him back, wrapping my arms around his neck as he pulled me closer. Our tongues mingled in a slow cadence that left me breathless and warm despite the bitter wind biting my exposed skin. He broke the kiss and leaned his forehead on mine.

"I have loved you for years," he whispered and closed his eyes. "I just thought I'd have time to change things before the gauntlet fell."

"But I'm just a servant girl," I said, wielding sarcasm like a sword.

"You shouldn't be," he said and glanced in the direction of the shimmering barrier. "You should be free, not enslaved to the regency." His eyes hardened as they looked through me. "You did not deserve what my mother sentenced you to."

He didn't know the half of it. When he kissed me again, I wanted to get lost in this minty bliss, but I knew better.

I pushed him away. "This is futile," I whispered under his lips.

"If I tell my mother..."

I bolted out of his lap, nearly stumbling into the stairwell hole. He caught my wrist, pulling me back to safety, but panic regarding his words kept my heart ramming into my ribcage.

"You cannot tell your mother," I insisted.

His eyes narrowed. "Still towing the greater good line?"

"No, I'm trying to save my mother's life!" My eyes went wide, and my hand flew over my mouth. Lightning sparked in the distance as I tried to calm my frayed nerves.

He blinked and his hands dropped from mine as he stepped back.

"Your mother threatened to exile her if I didn't help you accept her choice for the next regent," I said, glaring at him again. The fact this shit was spewing from my lips wasn't fully my choice. "Why are you making me spill my guts like this?" I yelled and stomped my foot.

His lips twitched into a smile and he shrugged. "I needed to know."

"You needed to know what?" I was seriously going to lose it. The night around me electrified in time with my volatility.

"I needed to know if I could trust anything you said or not. Or if you had been in league with my mother all along. I needed to know that this..." He pointed between the two of us. "Is real. Because if you feel like I do, then fuck marriage and fuck the sector. I choose you."

Fear layered with the frustration inside me, bringing forth more lightning. My gaze jumped to the sky when I realized my call to the elements earlier had somehow manifested in this building storm.

"I cannot watch my mother die," I said, forcing calm into my bones. I moved my gaze from the ominous sky to him. My self-preservation kicked in as well, and the storm slowly fizzled.

"Do you love me?"

I pressed my lips tight, refusing to answer, despite the overwhelming need to spill my guts.

"Do you love me?" he asked, clenching his hands into fists.

"Yes, you stupid ass. I love you!"

His mouth dropped open along with his hands. His eyes widened and then slowly closed as everything must have sunk in. When his eyes opened, a new determination lived there.

"I'll change my mother's mind."

"Your mother hates me. She would revel in seeing me suffer, and if she exiles my mother, all hell will break loose." I clamped my jaw against the rest, successfully keeping my magic a secret, for the moment. "What the hell did you give me?"

He pulled the mint sprig from inside his cheek. He glanced at it before he let the wind sweep it away. "I attempted a truth spell," he said with a shrug. "I guess I'm better at this shit than I thought, because I seem to have gotten some backlash of the magic, too."

"Why now?" I asked.

"Because I'm being forced into something I don't want, and I needed to know if there was something to fight for." He took a deep breath. "Why are you immune to my influence?"

I pressed my lips together against the answer straining to spill. Jaden stepped closer.

"Star?"

"Damn it, Jaden," I said, but my voice was as tight as my chest.

"Why, Star?" he pressed and pulled me closer.

Thunder rumbled and I stared into his eyes.

"My secret is as deadly as yours." The words squeaked out against my will.

A bolt of lightning traversed the sky overhead. Jaden followed my gaze, watching the chaotic lightning strikes all around us. A crease appeared between his eyes, and his gaze dropped to mine. With a cock of his head, the millions of questions I was sure flooded his mind reflected in the green of his eyes, but not one flowed over his lips. Not right away.

"Are you..." He dropped his hands and stepped back.

"Am I what?" I asked, knowing I was sealing my fate.

"A witch?"

I laughed and looked up at the sky. "What do you think?"

"I think you might be, but I can't figure out why you would hide it."

My gaze dropped to his. "Your mother had a conversation with my mom after she exiled my father. She said that if I ever showed a propensity for magic, she would destroy me. I guess your mother couldn't live with the fact my dad loved my mom and not her. He was sentenced to death because he told your mother to go to hell. It wasn't because he was a powerful witch. That was just her public excuse. It was because he refused her offer and chose to marry my mom."

Jaden's jaw dropped, and he started blinking like the information I fed him was short circuiting his brain. He glanced at the barrier, and he sucked his bottom lip between his teeth like he always did when he was processing. He turned his gaze back in my direction, and pain lived in his eyes.

I expected denial, but the words that came next shocked me.

"I wouldn't put it past her," he said, voicing the sad truth about how he felt about his mother.

"I'm sorry. I should have never..."

He put his hand up, stopping me. "Don't. You being brutally honest with me is my fault. I'm the one who mixed up a truth spell." His gaze traveled back to the barrier. It stayed there as lightning pinged the surrounding buildings, echoing my uneasiness. "Do you know what this means?" His eyes sparkled, and a smile surfaced.

"It means you have to marry someone else," I said. "Or both my mother and I die."

His smile slowly faded. "If I marry that woman, I'll be the one who is eventually exiled."

We stared at each other in silence. I kept my tongue. He would be safe. I made sure of that with the potion he drank before we started this crazy argument.

He stepped forward, threading his hands through my hair as he leaned in, delivering the kind of kiss I'd always dreamed of. Tender and sweet, but full of the desperation filling both of us. When his arms wrapped around me, the kiss deepened.

His hands traveled down my back until they cupped my ass, pulling me against him. The hardness beneath his jeans pressed into me, and my heart quickened. The dreams I had about making love to Jaden always took place here, in our sanctuary on top of the crumbling buildings, but it was never in the middle of the winter under a stormy sky.

I pulled away and stared into his eyes, wondering just how long the truth serum I ingested from that damn mint sprig would impact both of us.

"I want you," he whispered.

I let out a laugh. "I get that, but it's freezing." My teeth conveniently started chattering to amplify my point.

"I don't want to go back yet," he said, holding me in place.

"I know what you want to do, but it's too cold," I said and offered up a sly smile.

"So you want to find that empty room again and figure out what comes next?"

I hesitated because I could tell from his expression what came next. I wasn't ready to give him my soul. Not when he would be interviewing suitable wives tomorrow.

"You don't want me?" he asked, reading my hesitation wrong, and the damn truth serum compelled me to answer.

"I never said that," I said, successfully answering him without delving into my thought process.

"Then let's go talk," he said and stepped away, heading for the zip lines.

"But that's not what you want to do, is it?"

"Damn it," he mumbled and shook his head without looking at me.

I kind of liked the effects of his truth spell. "What is it you have in mind?"

He glared back at me and jumped, sliding down the rope before he had to answer. I followed after a moment, landing next to him and watching his lips press tighter together as if trying to keep the words from slipping out.

Instead of speaking, he slammed me into the wall, and his hand slipped between my legs just before his mouth found the curve of my neck. The way he teased me with a trail of kisses down to the v of my shirt turned on a fire inside like I had never experienced. The gentle rubbing of his fingers through my jeans suggested everything his silence did not.

"Jaden," I whispered, closing my eyes and letting his touch drive me to the edge.

When his fingers fumbled with my belt, I caught his wrist, holding it in place to stop this insanity. He pulled away, his eyes wide and nearly frantic with need. I shook my head, and his hand stilled between my thighs.

"You don't want this?"

Now it was my turn to curse at him. "Damn you. You know I want this more than anything," I said through clenched teeth.

"Then why deny me?"

"Because it will always be a rushed screw in a hidden room. It will always be forbidden," I whispered. Tears spilled from my eyes, creating hot paths down my cheeks. "It will never be what I truly want. I will never wake to you by my side, or go to sleep in your arms. I will never make love to you until the sun rises, and then make breakfast for us to eat in bed. These are things that cannot be, and if I let you lead me into that room, all I become is your mistress." I sniffled. "Your slutty little slave girl."

He stared into my eyes for an eternity and then slowly removed his hand from between my legs.

"I want you, Jaden. But I'll never have you," I said and took off down the stairs as the tightness in my chest formed harsh sobs. I stopped when I got to the lobby, torn between continuing to run or turning around and giving in to the visceral need to be with him.

His slow descent locked my feet in place, and I wiped my face in irritation. I wasn't this sobbing mess. I was better than that. Stronger than that. I had to be.

"You didn't leave." The surprise in his voice pulled a small smile to my lips.

"I couldn't."

"So you chose slutty slave girl?"

I allowed a huff of a laugh to escape. "No. I chose my best friend." I turned. "You are still my best friend, right?"

He closed the distance and took my hand. "Always."

We walked silently through the streets with our hands intertwined. I stopped when the Regent's sprawling estate came into view and pulled my hand from his warm grip.

"Promise me you won't say or do anything that puts my mother in danger," I said and looked from the homestead to him.

He sighed. "I promise as long as you keep my secret safe, too."

My lips twitched into a smile. "Mutual destruction."

He broke out in a grin. "I guess."

"So are you going to be a good boy and go interview that deranged fairy?"

"Only if you become my slutty slave girl," he said with a grin.

So, we were still at an impasse.

I sighed and decided to play coy. I gave him a deep curtsey and batted my eyes. "As you wish, my lord." I turned and gave him the bird as I walked away.

His rich laugh followed, and my heart ached for him.

Chapter 5

When I walked into the Regent's estate, chaos engulfed me. People ran like the house was on fire, their faces painted in portraits of panic. I took a few more steps and stopped, just staring at the utter madness.

The door opened behind me and I turned, meeting Jaden's gaze. He looked just as gobsmacked as I was. He crossed to where I stood, and before he could ask what was going on, I just shrugged.

Tasha, Samantha's personal assistant, popped out of nowhere and grabbed Jaden's arm, leading him away. "Oh, thank goodness you're back. Your mother was having an absolute meltdown."

He glanced back before she whisked him around the corner, and beyond the confusion in his eyes, there was a 'we aren't done yet' expression that chilled me.

I zigzagged through the bedlam, avoiding collisions as best I could until I got to the back section of the mansion and the servants' residences. Bypassing my room, I went straight to my mother's quarters. I knocked but didn't wait and stepped inside the modest accommodations.

My gaze landed on the red streaks crossing the floor. My heartrate tripled. I rushed into the kitchen, finding my mother on the floor.

"Mom!" I landed next to her, but she tried to push me away, leaving a bloody streak across my shirt.

"Stay back," she whispered. Then her body went into spasms.

I reached for her again to see just how bad she was hurt. At my touch, she turned towards me. I stumbled back at the mess that was her face. Blood ran from long gashes, and her left eye was completely closed.

"What happened?" I asked.

"Ravager," she said, her voice only a raspy exhale.

I blinked. "Where?"

She closed her eyes, and her head dropped to the ground. "Garden, tutoring Jack. Not a barrier breach," she whispered.

My heart sunk. Jack was Jaden's little brother. "Is Jack okay?" I leaned in close, but this time when she looked up, the virus had already started to take hold of her, turning her feral.

"Get away," she growled.

"Mom, please," I whispered.

She bared her teeth and hissed before climbing to her feet.

"I need to know if Jaden's brother is okay." My gaze dropped to her bloodied form. Her face wasn't the only thing mangled. A flap of skin hung from her chest, showing her ribs. The amount of blood coating her and pooled on the floor was too much. I had no idea how her body was able to sustain life.

"Run," she snarled as the ravager venom worked its black magic, turning her skin that dark grey that reminded me of death. Soon, she would be a mindless killer like those beyond the barrier.

My mind swirled and I blinked. A ravager inside the barrier meant a breach, but my mother just said it wasn't a breach. How could that be?

"What did you mean not a barrier breach?" I asked, praying there was enough of my mother left to get an answer.

Her door blasted open, making both of us jump. Jaden stepped inside with eyes as wild as my mother's. A bloodied sword hung from his hand. At the sight of my mom, he moved without hesitation.

"Don't!" I screamed.

But Jaden didn't listen. His blade whistled through the air, severing my mother's head from her body. Whatever changes had started, died with her, along with any logical explanation.

Numbing shock kept me in place. My gaze dropped to where my mother's head had rolled.

"Did she attack you?" Jaden spun towards me with the blade out in front of him, ready to strike again if he had to. His eyes scanned me, looking for injury that wasn't there, and the haunting pain reflected in his face relayed more than any words between us could. "Star! Did she bite you?"

His voice was brittle and harsh and jerked my attention back to him. I shook my head.

Jaden lowered the sword, letting out a shaky breath.

"You killed my mother." The words squeezed from my chest as reality slammed home.

"I had to kill my little brother, too." His voice was low and full of regret.

None of this made sense. I sat on the edge of my mother's kitchen bench trying to understand how things could devolve into such a catastrophe.

"There was a breach," he said.

I shook my head at where my dead mother lay. "She said it wasn't a breach."

He reached out for me, but I knocked his hand away. Reconciling the man I loved with the one who killed my mother with no hesitation didn't mesh in my head. I didn't need coddling; I needed answers. Answers he'd stolen from me.

"Star?" he said, his eyes now wide and sincere.

"You killed my mother," I said again, pointing.

"She would have killed you!" he argued. "She was turning into one of those beasts!"

I shook my head. "She was trying to tell me something before the venom poisoned her. And you just barged in here and decapitated her like she was the enemy."

"She was," he said. "Ravagers don't reason. They just kill."

I pressed my lips together as the burn of anger bubbled to the surface. "You don't know that!" I yelled at him, jumping to my feet and advancing as the need to knock him clear across the little efficiency apartment took hold.

The ground shook under us, nearly fracturing the walls in the room. A small part of me grasped for sanity.

"Get out!" I pointed at the door.

He opened his mouth to speak.

"So help me, Jaden, if you don't get out, I will hurt you," I snarled.

He stepped back, rising to his natural height, and his expression hardened. Without a word, he turned and marched out of the room.

The fury and sorrow mixed inside me to a level I couldn't contain. I dropped to my knees, letting scream after scream peel out of my throat until nothing came forth but a rasp in breath. I collapsed in tears on the floor, curling into a ball so I wouldn't have to look at my mother's severed head.

54

Chapter 6

"She's in shock," Jaden said, but his voice seemed far away.

I kept my eyes closed, wishing I had jumped from the tower and made the elements carry me away. At least then this crushing agony holding me captive wouldn't be ruling my world. My ability to speak, to tell them to leave me alone, was stripped by a prick of a needle in my arm.

"We need to burn the bodies," a voice I didn't recognize said.

No. I didn't want my mother burned and scattered like trash. I wanted to give her the proper burial ceremony and then send her ashes flowing on the breeze from my building hideaway in the city.

Medical officers lifted me onto a gurney.

"Jaden." His mother's sharp voice broke through the rest of the din. "What are you doing down here in the servants' quarters?"

Just the tone of her accusing voice made me want to curl in on myself.

"Her mother is the reason my son is dead," Samantha snapped. "She will pay dearly for her mother's transgression."

"No. Star is not to be punished," Jaden said with a tone as cold as the wind on the towers.

"Still protecting that little harlot?"

"I will always protect her, Mother. And stop calling her a harlot. We both know she's the innocent one here," he snapped.

With his words, my heart began to thaw.

"Your brother's death requires justice."

"Isn't her mother's death enough?" Jaden argued.

"I will make you a deal. You marry Eleanor, and I will reduce Star's punishment for her mother's sins," she said with such sweetness and venom that I nearly screamed, but my lips wouldn't open.

"That's not good enough, Mother. I will marry that deranged pixie of a girl only if you release Star from her servitude. Free her and promise not to harm her, and I'll do whatever you want me to do."

I wanted to open my eyes, but my eyelids were not cooperating. Nothing was cooperating.

Silence filtered over the room as everyone froze at Jaden's ultimatum. Seconds ticked by with my life in the balance of Samantha's whims.

"Fine. I release her from her parents' debt to the house of Mallory."

"And?" Jaden prodded.

"And I promise not to punish her for her mother's transgression."

"I want you to promise not to harm her. Ever," he said, low and insistent.

Another hush passed over the room.

"I promise not to harm her...ever," Samantha said, and I could tell it was through clenched teeth. "Now, your part of the deal. You will marry Eleanor this weekend."

"So be it," he said. "Thank you, Mother." His footsteps retreated until they faded altogether.

"Dump her outside. She is no longer my property. I will not provide her shelter," Samantha said.

"But, Regent..." the medic closest to me started.

"She no longer belongs here," she said, and there was no leeway in her tone.

When her footsteps faded in the same manner as Jaden's, the gurney rolled away in the opposite direction. I still couldn't speak or move from whatever drug they had given to me. My mother's body was probably being carted off to be burned with the day's garbage, and Jaden had promised to marry that witch. He sentenced himself to what he thought was a lifetime of misery just to set me free.

Hot tears burned the back of my throat, but none escaped. Not even when I was dumped in an alley outside the Regent's estate. Cold seeped from the ground, and the air wrapped me in a frigid blanket that I couldn't toss.

My entire form shivered, but my muscles were helpless to get me out of this frozen alley. My eyes closed, dipping me into a dark stupor.

"Get up, Star."

My eyes opened at the familiar voice.

"Get up and move," a vision of my mother said. She was enveloped in smoke, but it was her.

I forced my arms underneath me, pushing my face up and away from the frozen ground. "Mama," my hoarse voice whispered.

"If you stay still, you will freeze to death. Move, baby girl," the mist said.

This time when I mentally ordered my body to obey, it did, and I found myself on shaky legs, shivering. I wanted my warm bed and old comforter my mother knitted for me. I wanted my clothes and knickknacks I collected over the years. I turned towards the building, stumbling to the front entrance.

A guard I hadn't met before stepped into my path, preventing me from passing into the building.

"Excuse me," he said, putting his hand out. "What business do you have with the Regent?"

"I would like to retrieve my things from the servants' quarters," I said.

"Identification, please," he said.

I just stared at him. I had no identification on me. When I ran out earlier in the day, I didn't have a thing. I had never had cause to show identification when coming and going before, but then again, most of the regular guards knew my face.

"Well?"

"I'm sorry. Everything I have is in my room."

He raised an eyebrow. "The Regent has given the order that no one without proper identification is to enter the estate."

"But…"

He just shook his head, his expression turning hard. "No exceptions."

"Jaden Mallory will vouch for me," I said.

The guard's expression soured. "Ah, both the Regent and her son warned each and every one of us about you. They said you were unstable and would do anything to stop the marriage. Master Mallory does not want anything to do with you or your games, so I suggest you run along." He waved me away.

The cold wrapped her cruel hand around my heart, wringing the last drop of hope. I stepped back, unsure of what to do, but it was clear I wasn't going to get inside tonight.

"Jaden said he doesn't want…"

The guard gave me a curt nod.

I turned away from the only home I ever had. My feet knew the way through the streets to my sanctuary, even as my brain fogged over the events of the last few hours. When I stood in the lobby of our tall dilapidated skyscraper, I realized there was no solace here. No peace with it draped in memories of Jaden at every turn, but it was the only place I had to go.

I climbed the stairs, stopping on the seventeenth floor, then slipped through the stairwell door. Wind seeped between the broken windows lining the hallway to my left. I navigated the dark, trying to remember if it was the third or fourth door on my right.

Just because I was unsure, I opened the first door I came to and found the ragged remains of metal. Beyond the bent iron, a wall of window frames stood. The wind pushed the door back on me, and I let it close as my teeth joined in the shiver accosting my form. If I didn't find my room soon, I wasn't going to last the night.

The second resulted in the same as the first. When I stepped in front of the third door, I said a little prayer to the elements to help sustain me. Darkness blanketed me when I opened the door. It lulled me and I almost took that first step. Instead, I crouched and followed the doorframe down to where the floor should have been.

Closing my eyes, I sighed as my fingers passed the level of the hallway floor and my memory of the long dark shaft surfaced. If I had taken that step, I would have dropped seventeen floors, crashing to my death. And no one would have ever found me. Not even Jaden.

My heart jumped in my chest as I slammed the door closed. I glanced farther down the hallway, squinting to see where the next door was. Five paces and I stood before my last chance. I rested my forehead on the door and took a deep breath before I turned the knob.

The door blew open, and this time I did not trust the darkness. I licked my lips, trying to remember the rhyme my mother used to say when I was a kid and afraid of the dark.

"Goddess of the sun, make the dark become the light, help me make the sun shine in the night," I whispered holding my hand out in the dark. A moment later, a small spark danced over my palm, lighting up the space like a dim nightlight.

This was the room we had found on one of our adventures. It had four solid walls, a ceiling, and a floor. That was all I could hope for at this point, and while it was cold, it wasn't as frigid as the hallway. At least I would be sheltered for the night.

Holding my little light, I stepped inside and closed the door, looking for anything to provide warmth. My gaze fell on a metal rack stacked with reams of decayed paper. I couldn't be picky, not if I wanted to survive the elements. I dumped a few packages on the floor, containing any stray pieces that tried to drift off. When I had enough bedding down, I grabbed more paper, layering it on top of me as I lay down on my shredded bedding.

Exhaustion strangled my muscles. I curled tighter into a ball, shifting papers to cover me. Soon, my little space began to capture and keep my body heat, warming me to the point I wasn't shivering anymore. With the last of the paper reams tucked under my head, I closed my hand around the light, dousing it until blackness surrounded me.

With a quiet sigh, I let my mind still. Sleep didn't take long to arrive, and when it did, it plummeted me into a litany of nightmares. Nightmares filled with images of my burning mother, of Jaden's glare, and of Samantha's vicious laughter.

The door banged open and I jumped. My gaze flew around the room until it landed on a silhouette framed by the darkness of the doorway. I froze as a light shined in my direction.

"Star?" A voice drifted as the light scanned past me.

"Jaden?" I asked, sitting up. The papers covering me drifted to the ground.

He stepped in the room and closed the door. With the flashlight still shining in my eyes, I couldn't tell if it was Jaden or not. Fear collected in my belly until a familiar backpack dropped on the ground. The light moved away, but the shadows still darkened my vision.

Jaden knelt by the bag and set the flashlight on the floor so it washed the ceiling with light, creating a halo that illuminated the entire room.

"I kind of figured you'd end up here," he said without looking at me. "I'm so sorry. I didn't realize my mother gave the order to burn everything of yours, as well as your mother's, until I saw the pile of stuff outside waiting to be thrown into the bonfire." His lips pursed in disgust.

Instead of elaborating, he unzipped the backpack and pulled out the blanket my mother had made me. I pressed my lips together as mist clouded my vision, and then I forced the melon size lump forming in my throat into my fluttering stomach.

"I figured when I saw this, it was probably the one thing out of all the things in your room that you would need, for more than just warmth." He blinked away the sudden sheen covering his eyes while he spread the warm blanket over me.

"Thank you," I said with a shaking voice.

The next item he pulled out made me crack a small smile. I was instantly transported back to my bedroom on the night I broke my arm. Jaden had come by and given me a cute black and white stuffed bear to make me feel better. Now, he handed it over with the same sheepish smile he had worn then.

I slowly took it and hugged it to my chest.

When he pulled out a sundress, I raised an eyebrow at him.

"I have no idea. It was just there next to the blanket and the bear, so..." He shrugged and shoved the dress back into the bag. "That's all I could grab." He leaned back on his haunches and glanced at his watch.

"What's the hurry?" I asked through a rash of shivers that made my teeth click.

"I put some food and water in the bottom of the backpack along with a little money so you can at least get a coat or a change of clothes," he said, avoiding my question and any eye contact.

"Jaden," I said.

It took him a minute to meet my gaze. Again that same pain flashed, and he tried to give me a smile, but it didn't quite make it onto his lips. It certainly didn't reflect in his eyes.

"This is goodbye," he whispered.

All the air hissed from my lungs. A sucker punch to the gut would have been less painful. Hell, being decapitated would have been more pleasant than this crushing blow. I squeezed the bear closer to my chest like it could protect me from this utter devastation.

"You can't..." His fists closed, followed by his eyes, as he struggled to get the words out. "You can't come to the mansion to see me...and I can't come here again." He finally met my gaze. "I shouldn't even be here now."

"Why?" I asked, my voice as small as I felt. "What did I do that was so bad?"

His head dipped to his chest. "You didn't do anything," he whispered. "This is... This is just the way it has to be." His head snapped up, and resolve lived next to the pain on his face.

"So everything earlier was just a farce," I said, my voice carrying the edge cutting through me.

He slowly shook his head. "No. I meant everything I said, but it no longer matters. I made a choice."

"You chose to marry that little pixie in return for my freedom and my safety," I said, and he jerked like I had electrified him. "I heard everything. How could you do that? How could you agree to marry her?"

He looked up at the ceiling. When a tear traced his cheek, it was my turn to feel a jolt of surprise.

"You didn't hear everything," he said, and his gaze dropped to mine, his pain reflected as strongly as a shooting star on a clear night. "Unfortunately, my mother added an item...or two to the negotiations when she got back to her office. I have to publically denounce you, and I can never speak to you again."

Silence settled between us as he tried to somehow relay the magnitude of what that meant with his steady gaze. But I couldn't grasp what his silent communication was saying.

"Ever," he added when I didn't respond. His whisper was as morbid as the meaning behind that single word.

My mother's death had removed the stranglehold Samantha had on me, and as much as I hated it, the fact was the tragedy had a silver lining, or so I thought. But now all that came crashing down, and my body went numb from more than just the cold.

"Did you know your mother had me dumped in the alley like a piece of trash?" I asked, choosing the flare of anger swirling inside instead of the crippling devastation circling like a rabid ravager.

His head cocked, and a crease appeared between his eyes. "She told me you left. You refused medical treatment."

I let out a sarcastic laugh. "I nearly froze to death while I waited for that damn sedative to wear off." I didn't expand that it had actually been the ghost of my dead mother that got my ass moving. Instead, I glared at Jaden.

He covered his face with his hands, slowly wiping down until his eyes appeared above his fingers. "Maybe that was her hedge," he whispered, his voice shaking as much as his body. "Maybe she thought I wouldn't agree to her terms," he added and squeezed his eyes shut.

His blatant denial of his mother's horrific actions burned. "What will happen if you disobey?" I blurted.

His gaze lowered to the ground. "My mother will make me watch as ravagers tear you to pieces." He climbed to his feet and turned to leave.

He had no idea that I lived with that particular death threat every day of my life. Exile wasn't as devastating a thought to me as it clearly was to Jaden.

"Stay," I said. I jumped to my feet, dropping the bear on the makeshift bed. Desperation clung to my voice, and he hesitated at the door. I reached out, and the moment my fingers grazed his back, his chin dropped to his chest. "Please," I added, stepping closer.

"I. Can't." He barely squeezed the words out before he bolted out the door.

Based on the lumbering footsteps, I gathered he was running blind. I almost followed him, but the pain in his voice sliced through my resolve, shattering what was left of my heart.

I closed the door and retreated to my bed, trying not to let the thoughts overwhelm me, but that was already a losing battle. The center of my being felt as if someone had put a shotgun to my chest and pulled the trigger, leaving a bloody, gaping hole.

I swept the backpack off the ground and put it between me and the wall before settling down on my paper bedding. I hesitated to turn off the flashlight because with the absence of light came the despair that would fracture my soul.

With the bear hugged close to my chest, a steady stream of tears heated my face, soaking the only friend I seemed to have left.

I reached out from under the warmth of my mother's blanket and turned off the light, letting the darkness in.

Chapter 7

Sleep didn't come. I stared at the blackness surrounding me, fresh out of tears. I'd lost everything. My mother, Jaden, my home, and it all stewed right under the surface.

I replayed ever second of the last day and a half, wondering when the gods had decided my life should be ruined. The chips were falling long before I actually concocted the potion that would protect Jaden from harm.

I couldn't pinpoint the moment everything turned to shit. All I could think about was how warm and welcoming his lips had been. My chest hurt with the loss. Looking back, I reassessed every moment I had spent with the man since I turned thirteen. The hints he dropped were so clear on retrospect. Even the day he brought the bear to me under the guise that it was because I broke my arm, but there was more in that gesture, more in the gentle kiss he delivered to my cheek and the soft apology for not being there when it happened. All undertones of his true feelings and I had missed every single one.

I squeezed the stuffed animal tighter and stared at the darkness, beating myself up for my stupidity. Nine years worth of missed opportunities. Nine years worth of hints and actions that screamed his true intentions, but I was blinded by my station in life. Blinded by my mother's warnings. I always assumed everything he did was because he was my friend and nothing more. How incredibly shortsighted of me.

Perhaps this was a lesson from the gods. I never took the risk with my heart. I was too afraid of the consequences. Now, it was too late.

I was destined to lose him because of my inability to see beyond what I had been conditioned to see.

I rolled towards the wall, slinging my arm over my head to block the assault of memories. Sweet thoughts of his lips on mine, his hands claiming me in a way I never thought they would, turned bitter. I would never be with Jaden, romantic or otherwise, ever again.

"Damn it."

The hole in my heart widened as heat pooled in my eyes again. I squeezed my eyelids closed, willing the tears away.

My mind came back to the here and now, and the meaning he was trying so hard to convey to me started to seep in.

Denounced.

Jaden had to denounce me.

What kind of crap was that? Didn't he understand what that meant?

If he truly denounced me, my life was over. I'd be toxic to anyone who befriended me. This isolated room would be my only solace away from the persecution. I would be an outcast. A freed slave who had no future.

If that was the case, my choices were bleak. Live out my days in this room until I either starved or froze to death, or venture out into public only to be assaulted by whatever words came to mind of every passing stranger. In some cases, I'd heard the people get violent with outcasts, and more than once the sector had run someone through the barrier. It wasn't a life at all.

And as much as I'd like to see that pixie turn to dust, I couldn't set foot on the estate.

"Baby girl." My mother's voice surrounded me, lifting me from my self-pity stupor.

"Mama, just let me curl into a ball and die."

"I'm sorry. I cannot do that." Her voice wrapped around me with the warmth of the comforter.

I stiffened under the blankets and looked up into the glowing mist. "Why don't you move on? Why are you still hanging around?"

She crouched next to me. "You are not out of danger."

I rolled my eyes. Danger wasn't a new concept. All my life I lived with the idea that Samantha could smite me on a whim. "Mama, I love you, but you can't expect me to worry about Samantha Mallory cursing me or exiling me. I simply don't care right now."

She knelt in front of me, and her misty hand landed on my shoulder. "You need to care," she said, and her form wavered, like she was having issues holding on to it. "You need to watch your back."

"Fine." The need to appease that look of fear in her ghostly eyes made me bend to her will. "But you need to explain what you meant by not a breach," I said, needing to know exactly what that cryptic message was all about.

"They are closer than the boundaries," she said and then her form dissipated.

Frustration lined my throat, and I grumbled at the fact she couldn't hold on to her form long enough to spill the truth. Pulling the covers over my head, the air stilled around me, letting my body heat warm the small space. I chanced a glance from under the blanket to see if she had been able to reanimate. Unfortunately the only thing that ruled the room was darkness.

Little by little as the night burned into morning, the sunlight bled around the doorframe, announcing daybreak. This new dawn was accompanied by my rumbling stomach. Instead of trying to get any more sleep, I pushed myself up and reached for the backpack to see what Jaden had scrounged for me. With the flashlight whitewashing the ceiling, I pulled out the dress he packed and sighed as I held it up. A sundress with spaghetti straps was not made for winter wear. I folded it and set it aside.

Wrapped in napkins, I found a small piece of chicken and three of my favorite cream cheese brownies. I debated and re-wrapped the brownies, opting for the chicken. To the side sat two bottles of water and a folded piece of paper neatly tucked under the plastic.

I pulled out the water and just stared at the folded paper while I slowly ate the chicken. After washing my meal down with the cool liquid, I wiped my fingers and plucked the note from the depths of the bag.

Unfolding the paper, I stared at Jaden's elegant script filling the page. The date at the top gave me pause. This note was written a couple years ago, on my eighteenth birthday to be exact. I focused on the poem titled "Magic Star."

Every minute I spend with you is pure heaven...
Your eyes are a portal into ethereal light,
Especially when your smile shines,
And your silky hair blows in strands darker than night.
You are a magic I get lost in whenever your gaze finds mine.
Every night I see you in my dreams...
Finding solace in the softness of your lips,
I fall into your warm embrace,
Reaching ecstasy in the sensuous sway of your hips.
You are a magic I get lost in when rapture paints your face.
Every evening I wish upon a shooting star...

That the beauty I spend my days with will end up in my arms.

You are a magic I get lost in. Marry me, Star.

I stared at the note for what seemed like forever, and my mind drifted back to my birthday.

My mother had gotten the night off and invited a few of my friends to the pub in town for a celebration.

I had been laughing and dancing with Alex, one of the other servants who was my age, when Jaden walked in the pub. Our gazes met, and for a moment I thought I saw a flash of something dark glide across his features. I chalked it up to the lighting because a moment later, his easy smile surfaced, and he gave me a nod.

The backpack had been over his shoulder that night, and now I realized what that dark look was. Whatever he had planned had changed the moment he saw me swaying in Alex's arms. He hadn't given me my gift that night, either. If I recalled, he gave me a simple charm bracelet the next day.

I dumped the contents of the backpack on the blanket. What tumbled out shook the very foundation I sat on. I stared at the simple diamond silhouette sitting on top of the money Jaden had left in the bag for me.

With a shaking hand, I picked up the jewel and studied it, looking between the note and the ring in utter shock. The sheet of paper dropped from my left hand as I straightened out my fingers. The ring slid easily onto my ring finger, sitting snug enough to be considered a perfect fit. A lump formed in my throat, and my chest pounded with the level of pain gripping me.

Now I understood.

My life went off the rails the moment I insisted he marry another.

74

Chapter 8

With the money Jaden left me and a protection spell cast on my new space, I headed back into the heart of sector eleven.

The ring sparkled in the sun, but I needed something else—a dress for the celebration. For the wedding that should have been mine. As soon as I stepped into the marketplace, hushed whispers followed me, along with blatantly hostile stares and snide remarks that put me on edge.

By the time I ducked into the only formal dress shop in town, I was ready to tear my hair out or someone's face off. It was kind of a tossup. When I turned from the door, the entire place went silent. Wide eyes stared at me. A moment later when the door opened and a pixie witch stepped out in a wedding gown, I understood.

A saleslady hurried over, but it wasn't to greet me.

Her face was a mask of indignant disgust. "Please leave," she ordered loud enough for everyone in the place to hear.

I gawked at her and then ignored the saleswoman to cross to within a few feet of the witch Samantha had insisted on for her son. She was a few inches shorter than I was. By the narrowing of her eyes, she knew exactly who I was.

The saleswoman reached for me, but Eleanor put her hand up.

"Give us a moment," she said in the most annoyingly nasal voice I had ever heard.

When the staff and attendants stepped away, she moved closer, glaring up at me.

"The Regent warned all of us that you would try to somehow ruin this occasion. If you don't leave now, I will make sure you suffer until I choose to end your life."

I raised an eyebrow and crowded her, embracing my warrior persona. "I am not afraid of you," I snarled and glanced at her naked fingers. I smiled when I looked back at her scrunched face.

"You should be," she growled. "I'm a powerful witch," she added, puffing her chest like that should make me quake in my boots.

I kept my tongue about my heritage and leaned a little closer. "I heard you had some tainted blood in your gene pool."

The shocked blink confirmed my suspicion. There weren't many pure lineages left beyond the Mallory line and mine. My mother had once told me who in the sector came from pure blood, and this little deranged pixie wasn't on the list. I was surprised Samantha had chosen her to take over the Regency. Money and power seemed to be the deciding factor more so than the pure lineage bullshit, though.

"Who told you that?" she hissed.

Her indignant squeak pulled a chuckle from my throat. I had never been this nasty before, and a part of me cringed at the way I was treating this woman.

"Does it matter?" I asked, cocking my head in a challenge. "Besides, you don't really expect me to believe you love the Regent's son."

"I don't need to. Once I become Regent, he will be obsolete until I need to produce an heir." The arrogant bitch lifted her nose at me. "And then I'll have him jerk off in a cup."

I took a step back, unprepared for her candor or her spite. "What makes you think he will stick around?"

"I'll have his dick cut off if he lays a finger on another woman. And then I'll have the pleasure of feeding him to the ravagers myself." She flipped her hair back and pointed a finger at me. "And as for you, I lay the curse of the ages on you. May you..."

She didn't get the words out. Instead, my fist connected with her front teeth, knocking her on her ass. Blood dripped from her split lip, sprinkling onto the white of her dress. I grinned at my accomplishment. Eleanor would be getting married without her front teeth.

When her wail brought the staff running, I turned and bolted, but not before the witch issued the rest of her curse. Fortunately, I crafted a stronger protection spell before I left the skyscraper so I wouldn't be vulnerable to the Regent if I ran across her.

However, even with my protective barrier, the impact of Eleanor's spell nearly knocked me on my face. I stumbled, catching my footing before I continued running. I wondered if the curse bounced, or if it dispelled on contact. If it bounced, some poor soul would be the recipient of Eleanor's wrath.

I took the corner two blocks away and ran smack into someone coming out of a shop, knocking them over. I mumbled an apology and glanced up. Right into Jaden's amused green eyes. He was trying his best not to laugh and maintain composure, but the twitch of his lips gave him away. It was enough to jumpstart my heart, but it disappeared as quickly as it came.

He pushed me off like I was diseased and climbed to his feet. "Get the hell away from me." The glare he sent me set my teeth on edge.

"Fuck you, Jaden," I muttered as he turned away. I flipped my middle finger of my left hand at the back of his head.

He glanced over his shoulder and froze in place when his gaze landed on the ring. His eyes widened and snapped back to mine before they narrowed, and his lips tightened. This time there was rage accompanying his glare.

In that fraction of a second, I knew he didn't realize what had been in the backpack.

I didn't wait for a response. I turned and broke out in a sprint with my heart slamming my ribcage. My brain ran faster than my feet, trying to read exactly what his expression meant. Was he upset that I was wearing the engagement ring? Did he even recognize it as the ring he got me? Or did he think I was betrothed to another?

Too many unanswered questions fluttered through my mind, and I had no idea how to answer them. I waited until I saw the procession of Eleanor and her staff head back towards the mansion before I snuck back to the dress shop to see what I could buy with the money burning a hole in my pocket.

The bell rang, and the reception I received was even chillier than before.

"I need a dress," I said despite the glares.

"You will not find one at this shop," the saleswoman closest to me spit out and crossed her arms.

"I have money," I argued.

"Your money is no good here. As a matter of fact, I would think your money is no good anywhere in this sector," another sales woman snapped and pointed to the door.

My gaze crossed each and every face in the shop, and every single saleswoman held the same defiant disgust. Instead of holding my ground and insisting they let me buy something, I turned and left the bridal salon.

There were a few other stores that had dresses, but not ones for formal occasions like this one. Each store I entered had the same response. I grossly underestimated what being denounced by the Regency meant, and now the burn of the entire situation flushed my skin.

Chapter 9

The room in the tower seemed much less desolate now that I knew what my future held. A life of glares and being shunned lay ahead of me. I slumped on my paper bed, staring at the ceiling in the fading light from under the door.

I welcomed the dark, the solitude to get my head around everything that had happened.

But my solitude didn't last.

Jaden burst through the door, out of breath and as agitated as I had ever seen him.

"Who the hell are you engaged to?" he huffed and slammed the door behind him, engulfing us in the dark.

I flipped on the flashlight and shined it right in his eyes. I wasn't in the mood for his angry accusations or the hostility written in the set of his tight lips. So I reached into the bag and tossed him the folded note.

His eyes narrowed until he unfolded the paper. Even in the semi-darkness, his handwriting was hard to mistake for someone else's. He mopped his face with his free hand and leaned against the door.

"Holy mother," he whispered and closed his eyes. "You weren't supposed to..."

"To what?" I said when he didn't continue. "You want the goddamned ring back?" I yanked it from my finger and pitched it at him.

The note fluttered from his hand as he tried to intercept the flying jewelry, but it hit his chest and bounced onto the floor between us.

"Star," he whispered.

"Do you have any idea what today was like for me?" I snapped, ignoring the plea in his eyes.

"I didn't have a choice," he said with a little more strength.

"No. Don't you dare give me that absolute bullshit. You and that bitch of a mother of yours have made it impossible for me to survive in this sector. No one will let me buy clothing, whether it be fancy or regular. I wasn't allowed in any of the restaurants, and all the grocers turned me away. I had to eat a moldy piece of cheese out of a garbage can." Anger welled up inside, flashing over faster than I could control. Outside, thunder rumbled.

Jaden slowly slid down the wall until he folded into a sitting position on the floor. He crossed his arms on his knees and buried his face in the crook of his elbow.

I breathed, concentrating on not letting the winding fury take over my entire form. Each breath corralled the burning need to destroy everything around me, but when he looked up, that quizzical crease between his eyes nearly set me off.

"Why were you trying to buy a fancy dress?"

"I can't exactly show up at your wedding in this," I said, waving to my dirty clothes.

He picked up the note and the diamond ring in the center of the floor before he returned his gaze to mine. "You aren't welcome at the wedding."

"Then I might as well walk into a pack of ravagers," I growled at him.

He winced. "Don't..." His hands suddenly curled into fists, crumpling the note in one hand and palming the ring in the other. He looked up at the ceiling, taking slow breaths as if his own demons were getting the best of him, then he stood.

I climbed to my feet as well, bringing his attention to me. "Fuck you, Jaden. You've made it so I will not have any semblance of life. I will not know happiness or joy. I will never know love." My voice cracked, and I squeezed my eyes closed against the burn. "Congratulations. Your mother has won. She has destroyed my life."

He moved and before I knew it, he had me against the wall with his lips on mine and his entire body pressed into me. Electricity crackled between us, lighting up the room. It sparked from deep within my core, wrapping around us like a wild storm.

I didn't push him away. Even though the part that still had a sliver of dignity screamed not to let him in, I was helpless. This was all I'd ever have of Jaden. This moment, this intensity, this adoration in his eyes as he nearly ripped the clothes off me. My hands moved greedily of their own accord, stripping him of his coat, his shirt, his pants, until he laid me on my sad excuse for a bed.

He stared into my eyes, waiting for the rejection. Waiting for me to stop him from doing what he wanted. When I pulled him back to my lips, the kiss slowed into a sensual dream. His hands caressed my skin, and then his lips followed their path from my breasts to my core. He tenderly explored every inch of me, creating a burning heat in the center of my soul.

I tilted into his teasing mouth, his name exhaling in a satisfied moan.

Jaden kissed his way up my body, positioning himself between my legs. His eyes met mine, and he paused as if he was studying my very soul. The pulse between my legs nearly drove me mad. I wanted him. I didn't want this moment to be lost.

He must have read the need filling my body and soul because he slid inside with a slow thrust. I stiffened underneath him, my eyes widening at the sudden girth filling me, along with a flash of pain, breaking the last of my innocence.

He moved in a sinuously slow rhythm, driving away the pain with each stroke and replacing it with pleasure.

His eyelids dropped to half-mast, like he had taken a sip of his favorite fruit concoction. Bliss resided in the soft smile stretching his lips. When he whispered "Star," it was as if my name was the most precious word in the universe.

His rhythm increased, and energy pooled inside me, pulling from every cell, building until I arched my back and screamed his name as the wave hit. My fingers dug into his shoulders. Jaden's mouth covered my breast, teasing the sensitive nub, before he captured my mouth in an insanely intense kiss. Our tongues twirled with the same speed and force of our hips until he groaned, slamming his full length inside me.

He stilled, but his muscles trembled as much as mine. He pulled away from my lips and stared into my eyes, giving me a hint of a smile. "Every night I'll see you in my dreams... I'll fall into the memory of your warm embrace, relishing the ecstasy of your sensuous sway. You are a magic I'll get lost in every time I fall asleep," he whispered, paraphrasing the poem before he dipped his head to my shoulder.

When he wrapped his arms around me, I stared at the ceiling through a veil of tears as my hands slowly caressed his back, trying to memorize the feel of his skin. When I drew in a breath, I closed my eyes and cataloged the sweet smell of his cologne mixed with sweat and sex. All memories I wanted to last, all moments I'd never have again.

He pulled away and took my left hand, sliding the ring back on. "In case you need a reminder of where my heart truly is," he said and kissed my fingertips. He rolled off of me, and the sweetness of the moment soured.

I didn't want to move, didn't want to say goodbye. I pulled his dress shirt into my grasp, burying my nose in the fabric as he pulled his pants on. He turned to reach for it and stopped, raising an eyebrow.

I shrugged up at him. "I need a night shirt," I said, unwilling to let it go.

He crouched next to me and ran the back of his fingers across my cheek. "I didn't come here to..." He bit his lower lip and inhaled before he continued. "This was better than any dream. I now know what I'm missing, and it will kill me in the end." He pulled his hand away. "But at least we both know what it feels like now."

I raised an eyebrow. "You've never...?"

He chuckled and blushed bright red. "I've fucked before, if that's what you're asking, but that's not what this was." His fingers gently slid across my lips before he stood and pulled his coat on over his bare chest. "I've never made love before. I never put my soul into it, until now, and it was as beautiful as you are."

A lump formed in my throat, preventing me from responding.

He leaned down and placed a kiss on my forehead. "I hope you don't ever hate me," he whispered and straightened. "But you just might before all this is over," he added and turned, leaving me alone with the smell of him surrounding me.

Chapter 10

I woke in the middle of the night with darkness wrapped around me. Jaden's scent still clung to the shirt. I curled into a ball, letting it penetrate my senses. If I didn't have his shirt, I would have wondered if what had happened was real, or if it was just a vivid dream.

The slow realization that I was no longer a virgin also reared up through the fog. And the man responsible would be standing at the altar next to someone else in three days.

I had to find a suitable outfit because, despite what Jaden said, there was no way in hell I was going to miss the wedding. Not after what that witch said to me in the shop. I would relish seeing my protection spell in action.

I smiled in the black room, but it soon faded when I thought about trying to find a dress again. I had tried all the shops that only stocked new clothing. Now it was time to start looking at those second-hand shops that I always passed without another look.

With my plan of action in place, I huddled farther under my blanket and tried to catch a little more sleep before the day started in earnest.

* * *

The streets were crowded, so I tried to keep my head down to escape notice. I made it to one of the little shops on the edge of town without any interference. Inside, a dingy space held racks of clothing in a pattern I could not decipher. Men's clothing was combined with women's. I bit my nail, scanning for anything dressy.

In the far corner, I spied what I was looking for. As I crossed toward it, the curator came out of the back of the shop. Her flowing, floor length dress and her wild red hair, along with the flare with which she greeted me, categorized her as a free spirit, one who obviously hadn't gotten the memo that I was to be shunned.

"What can I do you for, girl?" she asked as she approached.

I shifted and eyed the dresses. "I'm looking for something appropriate for the wedding this weekend and some extra clothes to tide me over for a bit."

She raised an eyebrow. "You sure they will let a condemned slave into the gardens, missy?" Her arms crossed as she gave me a sideways glance.

My gaze dropped to the floor. I guessed the kind store owner knew who I was after all. I turned and took a step towards the door.

"Where you going?" she asked.

I paused and looked over my shoulder. "You obviously know who I am." I took another step away.

"Aye," she said. "Do you have money?"

I stopped again and nodded.

"I don't see many in this godforsaken sector offering to buy clothing from my store, so I'm not exactly in a position to turn away my next meal," she said.

"Really?"

The smile that graced her face filled me with a welcoming warmth. I flushed with gratefulness when she nodded. She rubbed her hands together and eyed me before she turned to the wall. She pulled two dresses down and held them out to me.

"You can try them on in the dressing room through that door," she said and pointed when I took the gowns.

In the dressing room, I slipped on the red frilly dress and glanced in the mirror. My nose wrinkled. This was not me. It had too many layers and was too girly. I slid it off and put it back on the hanger.

The other dress felt like a dream against my fingertips. Deep sapphire satin caressed my skin as I pulled the form-fitting dress over my head. The image in the mirror sent a pleasant shock through me. This dress fit like it had been made just for me.

I stepped out to model it to the thrift shop owner, and she beamed.

"That is perfect!" She clapped her hands with excitement and handed me a few pairs of jeans and some sweaters for me to try on.

I took the bundle and headed back in the dressing room. By the time I finished, I had a sizeable yes pile in comparison to those in the not my style pile. The only thing left that I needed were shoes for the dress and undergarments.

When I stepped out of the dressing room for the last time with the pile in my hands, I smiled at the row of sandals lined up by the bench.

"I took the liberty of picking out a few dress shoes for you to try," she said.

I began to worry about the cost of all these items, but I did need sandals because my worn boots would look atrocious with the blue dress. I reached for the silver sandals and slid my feet in. They fit just as perfectly as the dress, so I added them to my purchase.

The wad of money I pulled from my pocket didn't seem nearly enough to cover the pile on the counter.

"How much do I owe you?" I asked.

She eyed the money and pulled all but three bills from my hands.

"That should do it," she said with a smile and dumped everything in a fabric sack before handing it to me. "I suggest you try to take a bath before the blessed event."

I nodded. I knew I needed to clean up, but I had no idea it was so obvious that a stranger could pick up on it. Shame heated my face. A shower was something I took advantage of in the servant quarters of the mansion. Running water and decent facilities were not available to me in the high rise.

I mumbled my thank you and headed back into the crowded street.

A voice stood out among the rest. "Slutty servant girl."

I immediately recognized the owner. I glanced in the direction of the more upscale part of town, and there stood Jaden with Eleanor on his arm. Her lip was still discolored, and the gap where her teeth had been stood out with her sneer. Two massive guard dogs strained against the leashes she held.

A wicked grin formed. "Sick her, boys," she said with a lisp and let go of their harnesses.

My gaze met Jaden's and anger sparked inside me just as the dogs launched. I swung the bag as the first dog reached me. The beast dug its teeth into the cloth, ripping. The other dog joined in, yanking at the bag and tearing the contents within. I tried to pull it away, but they kept biting and tearing like it was a game until the clothing fell onto the road as ruined as the bag.

The dogs played tug-of-war with some of the items while Jaden wore an unfamiliar sadistic smile. But his eyes didn't match his expression. To me, they said 'run, get away.'

His wife-to-be was openly smiling, enjoying the humiliating show. "Kill," she commanded.

Jaden's eyes widened in horror, and his smile faltered.

I didn't wait. I turned to run, but before I was half a dozen steps away, the weight of one of her beasts connected with my back, sending me to the ground. Gravel bit into my palms. I shrugged my shoulders up to keep the dog from getting a grip on the back of my neck.

Rolling, I was able to knock the first dog off, but the second was on me in an instant. His fangs dug into my leg, yanking a yelp from my throat. The sky darkened above as my panic manifested.

A scream like a banshee came from the thrift store. The salesclerk came flying out with a broom, uttering an ancient hex that made the dogs retreat a few steps in confusion.

"Attack!" Eleanor yelled.

The dogs took a tentative step forward. The woman threw what looked like dust in their direction, and they backed off with their tails between their legs as if they had been sprayed by a skunk. The shop owner glared at Jaden and Eleanor as she reached her hand to me.

I took her offered hand, and she helped me to my feet.

"You arrogant ass," she snarled to Jaden and Eleanor. "Haven't you already done enough?" She put her arm around my waist and led me back into the confines of her store before the dogs were able to shake whatever she had thrown at them.

She clicked the lock and turned the closed sign so it faced out before she brought me into the back room behind the store. I glanced around at what appeared to be an efficiency apartment. It was bigger than what either my mother or I had in the servants' quarters.

I winced as she let go, and my full weight landed on my mangled calf. "I'm sorry, I'm bleeding all over your floor," I said, looking at the trail I left.

She had already stepped into another room. When she returned, she had a first aid kit in her hand.

"Don't be silly." She crouched down to tend to my wound. "My name's Gypsy Rose, by the way," she said with a smile as she cut my only pair of pants.

"Star Brighton," I said.

When she dabbed the puncture wounds with alcohol pads, I bit the inside of my lip to keep from wincing. She gave me a tiny smile and then stepped to her cupboard. When she pulled out a white candle, I let out a breath.

"You're a witch?" I asked.

"Aye." She lit the candle and set it down near my leg. "Magic mend and candle burn, heal this wound, and let good health return. By light of the moon and the path of the north, let infection be purged, and good health flow forth." She poured a small canister of liquid over my wounds. "Goddess of night, hear my humble plea, as I will it, so mote it be."

I gripped the arms of the chair as the liquid burned over each of the punctures. I didn't cry out, but the silent rant in my head was loud enough to drown out my panting breaths.

Gypsy wrapped my leg in gauze and gave my knee a pat before she put the candle on the small rickety table and slid into the chair opposite me. "Are you the one who knocked out her front teeth?"

My lips twitched into a smile at the same time heat filled my cheeks. I gave a single shoulder shrug in response. "I, um, I don't think those dogs spared any of the clothing I bought."

"I think that's probably a true statement, but I'm not going out there to see." She leaned forward and blew the candle out. The smoke drifted in my direction, forming a widening lasso before settling around me.

The smoky fog dissolved, leaving me lightheaded. I blinked and reached for the edge of the table. My leg started a maddening itch that reached down to the bone. I shifted. The world spun, and my eyes refused to focus.

The last thing that registered in my mind was the table coming towards my face at an alarming clip. Then darkness claimed me.

Chapter 11

I woke with a start, sitting up on a nice warm bed with my leg itching like I had stepped in a batch of poison ivy. The gauze was soaked, and I wasn't sure if that was the salve Gypsy had poured on it or if it was from whatever may be oozing out of the dog bites.

My caretaker wasn't in the little apartment. I swung my legs over the side of the bed. Testing to make sure my leg would hold my weight, I slowly stood and crossed to the doorway leading to the store.

Angry voices argued on the other side of the door. I leaned closer.

"Why does the Regent even care if I helped that poor girl?" Gypsy asked, her voice carrying exasperation. "What harm has she done to the Regent?"

"Her mother was responsible for the death of the Regent's son," a deep male voice snarled.

I almost stepped out in my mother's defense, but Gypsy's response gave me pause.

"So the girl must be punished for her mother's sins? How is that even remotely just?"

I leaned against the wall, thankful I found an ally, but Gypsy did not understand at all. I had been persecuted all my life, enslaved by a bitter and unstable woman just because my father had not chosen her. Lady Justice was blind in my case, and there was nothing that Gypsy could do to fix it.

"The orders stand. If you see her again, you are not to help in any way. Do you understand? No clothes, no food, no interfering with the Regent's wishes."

"She is not a criminal," Gypsy muttered.

"She is in the eyes of the Regent. This is a warning. If you give safe haven to the girl again, the Regent will see you tried and exiled."

I clenched my fists and hot tears burned my eyes and the back of my throat, but I wouldn't release them, not with the guard still in the building. As soon as I heard the bells above the door ring, I shuffled back to the bed and sat down.

Gypsy came into the room a few moments later, her cheeks almost as red as her hair. She pulled a chair out and took a seat with a sigh.

I stiffened, expecting the worst as she studied me.

"You overheard that conversation?" she asked, hooking her thumb towards the door.

I nodded and stood. "I guess I should be getting out of your hair."

"Sit down and rest that leg." She waved me back down.

I arched my eyebrows at her, surprised by her cavalier attitude to the threat of helping me. "But what about the guard's threat?"

Her hand fluttered back and forth like she was waving away a plume of smoke. "It's no bother. Samantha Mallory knows better than to challenge me. That woman has no power here."

My breath caught at her blatant disregard for the Regent. Especially since I had never heard of Gypsy Rose before I stumbled into this thrift shop. "What do you mean?"

"Our families have been at odds for generations. Unfortunately, I am the last of the Roses. Once I'm gone, there will be no one to remember or pass on the knowledge that the Mallory clan stole the regency from my family. They have poisoned sector eleven with their prejudices ever since. This is the first Mallory regency in over five hundred years that has not birthed a daughter." Gypsy smiled in a way that gave me chills. "It looks like the curse of my ancestors may finally have taken."

"What curse is that?" I asked. I didn't like the idea of Jaden being cursed at all.

"That the house of Mallory shall fall and another bloodline shall step in to rule. Unfortunately, it looks as if the next Regent is going to be even more heinous and cold-blooded than the current regime."

I huffed. Eleanor was shaping up to be far worse than Samantha ever was.

"Yes, she is. But Jaden isn't a bad person, so maybe he'll rub off on her," I said.

Gypsy laughed at me. "If he isn't a bad person, why did he just stand there and do nothing while you were being attacked?"

Things had moved so fast that I didn't have a chance to digest what happened. I had caught the plea in his eyes for me to run and the shock when that witch gave the kill order. The sparkle of the ring on my left hand captured my attention.

I knew why he didn't stop the dogs. It was the same reason why I didn't use my magic. We were in public and conditioned by fear.

"He's protecting me. If he lifts a finger to give me aid in public, I will be banished," I finally said, meeting Gypsy's eyes.

Her eyebrow rose, challenging me, but I kept the true nature of our relationship quiet.

"You think he's protecting you?" She cackled when I didn't answer her question. "That boy poisoned your reputation and made it impossible for you to survive in this part of the sector. You might be able to find somewhere up north to live in peace, but you won't find that here. Protecting you, my ass."

Most of the sector knew we grew up together and had a competitive streak. They had seen us racing down the street in a dead heat far too many times. But the sector didn't know we were the best of friends, and now lovers. I didn't know this woman well enough to expand any further than I already had.

"Well, let's see what we can do about getting you in shape for the wedding," she said, pulling my gaze to hers.

"Excuse me?"

"Just knowing they do not want you anywhere near the wedding gives me a good enough reason to make sure you are there."

Who was I to look a gift horse in the mouth?

I let a smile surface. "What did you have in mind?"

Chapter 12

I stood under the hot shower spray with my eyes closed, relishing the pelting beads of water massaging my shoulders. My mind remained focused on what Gypsy explained. Her plan was astonishingly simple, yet I knew there had to be some complexity in it. Just because she could give me a new hair color and make up my face so I wouldn't be recognizable didn't mean there would be challenges getting in.

My assumption was that the wedding would be by invite only, and not a general call to all citizens. As for Gypsy, she would be as likely to be on the invite list as I was, so we had to figure out what that invitation looked like in order to replicate it.

Not an easy task for two such outcasts.

However, the test run we were doing as soon as I cleaned up would give us an indication of how easy or difficult it would be to breach security on the big day. I just had to avoid Jaden. He, of all people, would recognize me. He would see under the facade.

I reached out and turned the spout off. My skin nearly shined, and the puncture wounds on my calf looked more like birthmarks instead of wounds. It was amazing just how refreshed I felt. I glanced in the mirror, and my skin was pink from the heat. I wrapped the towel around me. It reached from under my arms to just above my knees, and the plush softness encased me in a luxury I never would have thought this little efficiency apartment held.

I looked around for the clothes I had peeled off my body, but they were no longer in a pile on the floor. A chill crawled up my spine at the thought that Gypsy had come in while I was in the shower.

When I stepped into the main room, a stack of clean clothes sat on the chair near the bathroom door. I snatched them and slid back into the bathroom to dress. The soft silky fabrics caressed my skin. I studied the outfit in the mirror. It wasn't my usual t-shirt and jeans. This was more upscale, more sleek.

A soft knock sounded. I quickly hand-combed the knots out of my hair then reached for the doorknob. Gypsy stood on the other side with a grin and one of the largest makeup bags I'd ever seen.

"Are you ready for your transformation?"

I took one last glance at my face and then gave her a nod, following her out into her little apartment. She waved to the chair my clothes had occupied, and I took a seat.

Gypsy started with my hair, combing it. The sleepy lull she created with each stroke of the brush sent relaxing tingles though my body until I was in a state somewhere between awake and slumber. The comb caught on a knot, yanking me back to full awareness with the scream of my scalp.

She continued without so much as a pause, separating sections and rolling them into small curls that she pinned to my head. The number of times she pricked my scalp with bobby pins gave me an indication of just how many mini-rolls of hair sat on my head. I couldn't see the result, but I thought I must have over two dozen of these mini-buns stuck in no semblance of order.

I started to doubt her hairstyling abilities. That's when she stepped in front of me, surveying her work. With a satisfied nod, she opened her parlor bag and pulled out lotions and powders galore, then lined them up on the shelf in an order only she could discern.

The silence was killing me. "Tell me about what happened with your family," I said, then added, "If you wouldn't mind."

She paused and stepped back, meeting my gaze. "You took history in school, didn't you?" she asked, but her tone wasn't mocking or sarcastic at all.

I nodded. She raised an eyebrow, challenging me.

"They taught us about the wars that nearly destroyed civilization and the fight for survival after that, especially with the ravagers overrunning the world. They said the ravagers came from some sort of viral mutation, and after seeing what happened to my mother, I'd have to agree." My gaze fell to the floor, and I shuddered at the memory of the dark grey mass creeping like an army of ants over her deathly pale skin. I took a deep breath, trying to shake the image before I spoke again. "I guess the council of witches decided enough was enough and overthrew what was left of the existing governments. In order to preserve humankind, they created sixteen sectors far enough apart to keep each of them safe. Now, if the magic protecting one sector fails, the rest would still survive."

She slowly nodded as I spoke.

"Is what they are teaching accurate?" I asked in a hushed voice. I always wondered how much of history was real and how much of it was made up to align with the arcane rules we had in place.

"That much of the history is true. However, what came before the great divide is when my ancestors got slighted. When a seat on the High Sixteen became available, my ancestral grandmother from the house of Rose was being considered, along with a witch from the house of Mallory. Instead of playing by the rules and doing an honest display of her breadth of magic, the witch from the house of Mallory poisoned my grandmother, tipping the scales in Mallory's direction. The poison not only diluted my grandmother's power in the trials, but it pushed the boundaries of her mortality, dropping her into a deadly slumber. She woke just long enough to tell her kin of the subterfuge. By the time they attempted to step in, the sectors had already been defined, and the house of Mallory was put into rule over sector eleven.

"That was when her kin put the curse on the house of Mallory. I think they meant for it to take hold right away, but something must have gone wrong because the house of Mallory has produced a female witch in every generation until now. And because Samantha Mallory couldn't produce a female heir, it looks as if the house of Mallory will finally fall." She gave me a haunting smile. "At least I will get to see that before I pass on."

A chill settled in my bones, and I tried not to shiver. "So, what is with the 'get married before twenty-five' thing?"

Gypsy laughed. "One of the most asinine rules that the house of Mallory put in place." A shadow crossed over her face, and she glanced away. "That bitch lured my one and only love out of my arms and into a loveless marriage with all sorts of promises that fell short. She gave birth to that arrogant brat, and then the only man I ever loved died of some mysterious disease." Her lips thinned to barely a line as she dipped her hand into the bag and pulled out more of her powders. She started working on my transformation again.

I didn't dare correct her slight of Jaden, not with the anger blazing in her eyes. Her obvious hatred of Jaden reminded me of Samantha's hatred of me, and I had to wonder if there was a parallel between the two women.

"It took her almost fifteen years before she decided to go on the prowl again. From what I understand, she bedded a simpleton in the north country when she was on vacation that year. Her little escapade backfired, and she got knocked up. Perhaps she was hoping for a natural heir, but what she got was a second boy. A child just as sweet as his father supposedly was, but who carried not a stitch of common sense." She brushed my cheeks. "Or so I heard," she added, meeting my gaze.

"Jack was a sweet boy," I said, affirming her assumption, and she seemed to soften. This time, when she resumed her art, I remained quiet, letting her do her thing.

After a few minutes of primping and preening, highlighting and shading, I asked the question that kept circling in my mind. "Do you think the other fifteen sectors are still in place?"

The brush on my eyelid paused, and she gave a slow, long sigh. "I certainly hope so, but who knows. I remember my mother telling me that there had been a visit from a high witch from one of the other sectors when she was young, but that was over a century ago."

I met her gaze and then looked down so she could continue shading my eyes. The brush tickled my skin, but I forced myself to remain still and stoic. When Gypsy finally stepped back, I opened my eyes, trying to figure out if her expression was one of satisfaction or contempt.

She grunted with a curt nod and stepped close, unrolling all the mini-buns in my hair.

When a corkscrew curl fell into my eyes, I huffed at the pink and blue hues.

When she had finished, my raven hair was now a wild array of colors. I had only seen hair like this once, and that was at one of the Regent's balls. I glanced at Gypsy through the rainbow, and she swept most of it back into an up-do of some sort. When she finished and waved for me to take a peek in the bathroom mirror, I stepped in front of the looking glass and stared.

I did not recognize the woman staring back at me. She was stunning beyond compare, with the creamiest complexion I had ever seen, adorned with pouty red lips, and dark eyes made bright by colorful eye shadow. The hair complemented the entire look. I glanced at Gypsy, amazed at the transformation.

I doubted anyone at the mansion would recognize me, not even Jaden. Hell, my mother wouldn't even recognize me if she were alive.

"I'm impressed."

"Now for your new identity," she said and handed me a sheet of paper. My picture stared back, along with the name Amber Briar and an address from the eastern shore.

"Now what?" I asked, following her back into the heart of her apartment.

"Now, you're almost ready to request a meeting with her majesty."

I laughed. "And why would I do that?" I knew I was going to go by the palace, but I had no idea Gypsy expected me to enter and request an audience with Samantha Mallory.

"It is the only way you will get an invitation to the wedding."

I blinked and looked down at the paper again. Being invited and sitting with the guests was a hell of a lot easier than trying to sneak in. And it was eons better than watching from the branch of one of the trees outside the estate wall.

"I'm not sure I follow."

"You will enter and gush about how the news of her son's wedding has spread all the way over to the eastern shore quadrant, and you came all the way down here in the hopes to see a royal wedding." She smiled at me. "Gush and compliment her, the estate, and anything else you can. She will give you an invite just to get you out of her hair. But first we have to teach you to talk like an easterner."

"What's wrong with the way I talk?"

"Nothing if you're from the south side of the sector, but the eastern folk talk a little different. Their r's are softer. We say we're going to the park. They say they're going to the pahk. The r almost becomes silent when it is contained within a word and follows a vowel. So proud would still be proud, but bar is bah, and oar is oah, and softer is softah."

I tried to remember any of the eastern shore visitors over the years, then glanced at the name again before adopting the persona Gypsy wanted from me.

"Hello, I'm Ambah Briah. I'm from the eastahn shoah, and I'm heah to request an audience with the Regent." I extended my hand and flashed a winning smile.

Gypsy's eyebrows arched, her mouth popping open.

I grinned. "You thought I was a little on the stupid side, didn't you?"

She let out a small laugh, her cheeks flushing in response. "Well, I had heard you were a bit daft."

"There were some things my mother and I kept from the Regent. One of them was just how far from a dimwit I actually am."

"You are full of surprises."

She reached into the closet, pulled out a more formal pea coat, and extended it to me. Between the upscale clothing and the coat, I was almost ready to go, but both our gazes dropped to my stocking-clad feet. She snapped her fingers and stepped out the door into the thrift shop, then came back a few minutes later with a pair of high-heeled boots.

By the time I slid both feet inside and zipped up the fine leather, the knot in my stomach had tightened to an almost unmanageable level. If anyone doubted my identity…

I closed my eyes, taking another deep breath, this time to calm my fraying nerves. For all I knew, I was walking to my death today.

Chapter 13

The chill in the air swept over my cheeks. I crossed the street, clutching the small hand purse that Gypsy sent me with. She sat in the cafe across the street from the Regent's estate and had instructed me to walk like I owned the entire town, like I had a right to enter the premises. Despite my thumping heart, I did exactly as instructed, taking advantage of the fear and turning it into a visible excitement.

I stepped through the gate, and the guard immediately put his arm out, stopping my progress before he stepped in front of me. I looked up into familiar brown eyes. Cameron Hinkle looked down on me with a perplexed glare.

"State your name and your business with the Regent," he said in that overly formal manner I had heard for years.

I smiled. "I'm Ambah Briah," I said as if he should know who I was. When he just raised an eyebrow, I continued. "I'm from the eastahn shoah and I'm here to request an audience with the Regent."

"Identification, please?" He held his hand out, waiting.

I pulled the papers out of my clutch and handed them to him, keeping the smile on my lips. I glanced towards the mansion, gawking like Gypsy told me to as he stepped into the guard station. When Cameron stepped back from the small alcove, he handed me the papers and nodded towards the house.

"Regent Mallory's assistant will meet you in the entry."

I beamed and stuffed my papers back into my purse. I nearly skipped to the door, exuding as much enthusiasm as I could muster. When I stepped inside, I widened my eyes and took in the grand entrance to the mansion like I had never seen it before. The architecture always had impressed me, but pretending this was the first time seeing the grandiose entry was interesting.

"Ms. Briar?"

A voice to my right called my attention away from the marble-lined staircase. I turned, facing another familiar face. Tasha had seen me at least a dozen times a week when I was serving the Mallory family, but there was no hint of recognition in her eyes.

"Yes," I said and offered my hand.

Tasha took it and gave it a quick shake before she waved me to the right of the entry into the wing with the offices.

The moment we stepped into the hall, my gaze landed on Jaden. His gait slowed as he stared at me. I met his stare and plastered an overwhelmed smile on my face. I didn't know whether to curtsy or bow at the sight of the Regent's son, so I did some sort of half-assed combination.

"S—Sir Mallory," I stuttered like all the nimble-minded fan girls did whenever they saw him in the street. My heart thundered in my ears as I prayed to the elements for him not to recognize me.

"Miss," he said, giving me a head nod, but his gaze lingered, taking in my entire form before he gave me a hint of a smile. The spark of interest in his eyes almost made me lose my concentration.

"Ambah Briah," I said and stuck my hand out as if I remembered my manners.

His dimples made an appearance, and I thought for a moment he knew it was me. He accepted my hand and made a grand gesture of kissing my knuckles.

"Nice to meet you, Miss Briar," he said.

I knew he was just as clueless as Tasha and Cameron had been. I had seen him do the same thing to countless visitors. If he knew it was me, he would have just accepted the handshake and not done the formal greeting that his mother insisted upon. He left us standing in the hallway staring after him.

"His fiancé is a lucky woman," I whispered to Tasha, giving the impression of almost swooning at the attention of Jaden Mallory. Inside, my eyes were rolling.

She gave me a tight smile and continued to lead me to the Regent's office. With Jaden as clueless as he was, my confidence in the Regent not identifying me solidified. Although, I still didn't know how to get a wedding invite out of the entire thing, or what the hell I was supposed to gush about.

Tasha pushed the door open and led me inside. Samantha was engrossed with something in the papers laid out on her desk. She didn't bother looking up until Tasha cleared her throat.

Samantha raised her gaze, taking the two of us in. I let my eyes wander around her beautifully designed office as if I was seeing it for the first time. When my gaze returned to the desk, Samantha was standing and quietly studying me.

"Oh, I'm very sorry, Regent. I didn't mean to be rude, but everything I've seen since I've entered your home is impressive." I flashed a smile.

She gave me her tolerant expression. "May I help you?"

Heat filled my cheeks, and I shifted my weight. "Word of the wedding prompted me to come. I have always dreamed of seeing a royal wedding in person..." I dropped my gaze. "It might have been a little presumptuous of me to come all this way, but..."

"Where exactly are you from?" she asked.

"Eastern shore country, your Regency," I answered, hoping I hadn't unintentionally lost the accent.

She raised an eyebrow. "You got here awful fast, considering it has only been a few days since my son agreed to be married."

Gypsy had walked me through this line of questioning, so I just nodded.

"Yes, ma'am. One of the local witches had a vision. She heard of the search for a suitable witch and was hoping she was in the running." I rolled my eyes, opting for something more brazen than a wide-eyed, fan girl. "After she said someone was going to be chosen, I left the next morning."

"And you expect me to believe that you walked here and still look like that?"

"No, ma'am. I'm a woman of means. I arrived a couple days ago, just in time for the announcement. It took me this long to get up the nerve to come see you." I folded my hands in front of me. "You see, I'd like to build a career planning weddings when I get out of school, but I haven't had the chance to see a fancy wedding, at least not one like the scale of a royal wedding, and I thought this would be a great opportunity."

She studied me with narrowed eyes. I projected what I thought was the right level of nerves, biting my lower lip as she weighed her decision.

She stepped around the desk, approaching me in a predatory way meant to intimidate.

"A wedding planner?"

I met her gaze and beamed a smile. "Oh yes, your Regency. Planning weddings is my passion. The flowers, the meal, the music—it all must be done in a concert of timing and flair. When done well, no one knows any different, but when it isn't, the most significant moment of someone's life can be ruined by the ineptitude of the planner."

She looked over my head at Tasha. "Do you agree with Miss Briar?"

"Yes, ma'am. A well planned event is seamless."

The Regent looked down at me.

"I want to see what a perfectly planned event looks like," I said, playing directly to Samantha's vanity. "Up close."

She nodded slowly. "Well, then, Tasha, see to it that Miss Briar has an invitation." Her eyes pierced into me. "And then after the event, I would like to hear what you thought of the presentation."

I smiled. "My pleasure." I gave a small bow of my head, showing my respect. "Thank you," I added but didn't leave my spot.

"Please show Miss Briar out," she said and returned to her desk.

"Yes, ma'am," Tasha said, and I followed her out of Samantha's office. She stopped at her desk and pulled out an invitation, handing it to me. "I am planning the wedding."

I gave her a smile. "Then I'll be sure to not give any bad feedback."

Tasha blinked at me and cocked her head.

"It's the least I can do for you since you control the Regent's schedule and allowed me an audience with her," I said.

It was common knowledge that the Regent's personal assistant controlled Samantha's visitors' schedule. No one got into the Regent's office without Tasha's say.

She smiled and a blush brushed her cheeks as she stepped away from the desk. The minute we walked into the hall, Eleanor passed us without so much as a glance. She stalked straight into the Regent's office. I caught the sour expression on Tasha's face, but I kept my peace and followed her into the grand entry.

"Thank you," I said and offered my hand. She shook it, and I walked out of the building.

"Do I know you?"

I jumped at the sound of Jaden's voice and nearly tumbled down the stairs. He grabbed my arm and pulled me to his chest to prevent me from falling. I met his gaze, and my breath caught.

Time stood still, and we stared until I blinked and came to my wits.

"Thank you," I said and stepped away. "And no, we haven't met before today."

He grinned, and that sparkle returned to his eyes. "I just have this nagging feeling that I should know you."

I refrained from rolling my eyes and shrugged. "I certainly would remember speaking with the Regent's son. Hell, I'd be the envy of my entire town if they knew I was talking to you right now." I laid it on as thick as I could muster without gagging on my words.

He laughed in that rich baritone that made my heart quicken. In the back of my mind, I wished he would just call me out. But he didn't. Instead, he took my hand and brought it to his lips again.

This time it was my left hand, and as he pressed his lips to my skin, I felt the electricity building between us. He opened his eyes, and his gaze landed on the ring.

He froze, but he recovered faster than I did. I had forgotten to leave the ring behind. Recognition flashed in his eyes, and my throat tightened. That spark of intrigue turned into a fiery anger. He let go of my hand and stepped to my side as if he was going to pass me.

"Star?" His whisper hit my ear.

"It was nice meeting you," I said, glancing his way before I climbed down the steps.

The spot between my shoulder blades burned, but while every fiber in my body wanted to turn to see if he was still staring at me, I refused to give in to the sensation. I didn't turn. Not even when I entered the coffee shop across the street.

My heart was pounding so hard, I didn't hear Gypsy ask how it went. I collapsed in the chair next to her, still lost in the feel of Jaden's hand and the whisper of his voice saying my name. I closed my eyes, remembering ever moment.

"Well?" Gypsy's shrill question drilled through my reverie.

I glanced at her before opening my clutch purse and pulling out the coveted invitation. "You just have to do this magic again, and we will be able to go to the wedding."

Gypsy's grin reminded me of a picture I had seen at the old library. I think it was called a shark. They tore their victims to shreds, and I was sure Samantha would do that to me if she ever found out about my ruse.

If I recalled correctly, a shark used to be one of the world's greatest predators.

That is, until the ravagers came into existence.

STAR CROSSED

Chapter 14

"I knew your mother when we were younger," Gypsy said.

I looked up from my warm soup. Ever since I got the invitation to the wedding, I hadn't been a great conversationalist. Especially since all she could talk about was the pending nuptials, which was the last thing on earth I wanted to discuss.

My skin prickled. "You knew my mother?"

"Yes. She was such a sweet thing. Smart and beautiful, and destined to lose her soulmate one way or another." She sighed and slurped the last of the soup from her bowl.

"Why do you say that?"

"Because once a man has the Regent's attention, it's like the kiss of death. Samantha

Mallory targeted your father the minute my love passed away."

I knew enough of what happened as soon as the Regent decided she wanted my father. I didn't need to hear it again from the mouth of a virtual stranger. While Gypsy had given me safe haven for the last couple of days, I wasn't ready to call her a friend or spill my secrets to her just because she made me feel safe. The hostility she harbored against Jaden gave me pause, and I wondered if I would ever be able to let my guard down. The thought was sobering and exhausting at the same time.

"I don't want to be rude, but I really don't want to discuss what happened to my father. It still burns," I said, opening up enough to not feel like a complete freeloader.

Gypsy gave me a nod as if she understood. "Well, then, I am very excited for tomorrow. I have procured the perfect dress for you to wear, and I cannot wait to see it on you."

I gave her the same weary look. Except this time, she ignored me and continued to rattle on about all sorts of wedding related news, including undertones of hostility the staff at the estate had witnessed between Jaden and Eleanor. She seemed to thrive off the thought of his lifelong misery.

The more she talked, the more uneasy I became. What if my spell didn't work? Jaden would be harnessed to that royal bitch for the rest of his life. I couldn't stomach that thought either.

I forced a yawn. I had scrubbed Gypsy's little efficiency from top to bottom this morning while she worked in the shop. She had been pleased, but the exertion of cleaning sucked the energy from my bones. All I wanted to do was go to sleep and forget what tomorrow held.

She paused and gave my head a pat as if I was a small child before she stood and cleared the dishes. "Why don't you get some rest? Tomorrow is going to be a big day."

"I think that's an excellent idea," I said and cleared the rest of the table. The mat and sleeping bag she let me borrow were near the closet and I rolled them out where I wasn't in her way. With a tired nod, I headed into the bathroom for my nightly routine of cleaning my teeth and brushing the knots out of my hair.

I settled inside the warm sleeping bag and thought about my mother's comforter. I needed to get that one of these days, especially if this arrangement with Gypsy continued on after the wedding.

"I wanted to thank you for your kindness," I said and gave Gypsy a tired smile.

"It's the least I can do," she said and stepped into the bathroom to begin her usual bedtime custom. I closed my eyes, hoping she would buy the ruse when she came out and hush up for the night.

Darkness engulfed me, and I never even heard Gypsy come out.

"Starlight..." A soft voice invaded my mind, and I opened my eyes to the same mist I remembered from the alley.

My mother smiled down at me and crouched so she could reach out and touch my cheek. The warmth in her fingertips soothed my form.

"Star bright..."

She gave me such a sad smile that my heart hurt.

"Baby, you need to heed my warnings. The Regent has plans for you. Dark plans. Horrific plans," she whispered, before her voice trailed to nothing, and her form started to fade.

"Mamma?"

Her fading form seemed to solidify at my acknowledgement. "It wasn't a breach," she said and stood, her hands in fists as she tried desperately to cling to this realm. "Monsters lay within..."

"Within what?" I asked, but she was already flowing in the wind.

"Stay away from him..."

The last whisper sent chills through me.

"Who?"

But she was already gone.

I stared into the darkness, now wide awake with every cell pounding with unease. I already knew who she meant. Jaden. She wanted me to stay away from Jaden like she always had. I didn't understand why she would come with the same tired warnings, so I rolled onto my side, away from where she had drifted off.

But sleep didn't come for some time, and when it did, it was filled with the most heinous dreams of blood and pain and despair.

Chapter 15

Jaden's *getting married today.*

The thought kept circling in my head as Gypsy did her magic with my hair and makeup once again. I tried not to fidget, but I couldn't help it. I was as nervous as if this was *my* wedding day.

I wondered if the spell I cast would work. I wondered if the spark of anger I had seen in Jaden's eyes on the palace steps was aimed at me or my stupidity for tempting fate. I wondered if he still cared at all.

My gaze dropped to the ring on my hand and I sighed. The diamond on my finger meant I had his heart, but it certainly didn't feel that way. I closed my eyes under Gypsy's primping, and the vision of his sparkling gaze filled my mind. I could almost feel the caress of his fingers across my skin.

"There," Gypsy said.

I nearly ran to the mirror in the bathroom to see if I looked half as impressive as I had the other day. Amber Briar looked back with that same flawless skin as before, but instead of a chic up-do, my hair cascaded down my back in a rainbow of waves.

Gypsy walked in with a royal blue chiffon and satin gown with a silver-beaded, crisscross shoulder strap. The beaded accent continued to the waistline where it ended in a beautiful floral pattern. The skirt had a deep slit that would help show off the silver beaded heels she handed me. The dress was gorgeous.

"Seriously?"

"Try it on," she said and left me to slip on the silky gown.

It hugged my curves and showed more skin than I was comfortable with, but I had to admit the combination was stunning. I strapped on the shoes and stood back with a critical eye. Even with the amazing makeup job, I still thought my nose was a tad too big and my eyes were set too close.

With a sigh, I opened the door.

Gypsy looked up from the table, and a slow, evil smirk appeared. "I have a feeling you just might cause a scene."

I flashed an uneasy smile as she grabbed a coat for each of us. I glanced at the less than flashy clothing she wore and raised my eyebrow.

"I'm your guest, your great aunt Gypsy Rose."

"Is Amber really your niece?"

Her grin widened. "Yes. Otherwise, you would not have made it into the estate."

"Ah. And Amber is a struggling wedding planner?"

She nodded. "The girl would have loved to come to see the wedding, but she can't leave the eastern shore. For some reason, the city gives her hives."

I laughed under my breath. "Exactly how long have you planned this elaborate scheme?"

"The minute I heard of your mother's death."

My arms turned into a relief map of bumps. The shock of her words left me wondering whether I was a pawn in her game, or if she was truly trying to help me. I quickly shrugged my arms into the coat she had handed me.

"Does the Regent know that Amber is your niece?"

"The Regent has a complete list of my relatives."

I stopped at the door. "Are you setting me up?" The question tumbled from my lips before I could catch it, but I had to know. I glanced over my shoulder, willing Gypsy to be honest with me.

"No, child. I'm trying to help you see what a curse the Mallorys are. The only one that seemed to have a decent heart was killed at the same time as your mother, and I'm not sure it was an accident."

"A ravager attacked them." My mother had said it wasn't a breach, and at some point, I had to look into that, but right now I was worried about Jaden.

She hooked her arm around mine and led me out the door. "So I hear, but if a ravager breached the barrier, I would think there would be a trail of dead bodies between the breach and the Regent's mansion."

Gypsy had a point. I digested her words as we walked. The closer to the estate we got, the more my heart clanged in my chest. The chill in the air barely registered on my exposed skin. The minute we crossed through the gate, we were stopped. I flashed the invitation from my clutch, and the guard, who I had never seen before, studied the piece of paper and then handed it back without a word, waving me inside.

I honestly didn't think it would be that easy. We followed the crowd to the grand garden where the weather had been manipulated to a warm spring day. One of the butlers was taking guest coats, so I added mine to the pile with a polite thank you.

Jaden stood to the side talking with a couple of his friends, but the minute his gaze traveled by me, it snapped back. That spark of recognition lit in his eyes. After all, I was wearing the same glamour I wore the other day. His blatant stare made his friends turn and look in my direction as well. I had never felt so exposed with three sets of eyes mentally undressing me.

Heat filled my cheeks. I acknowledged Jaden with barely a nod, and he blinked and resumed whatever conversation they had been engaged in. I glanced at Gypsy, who studied me with a deep crease between her eyes.

I shrugged. "I guess maybe I am sort of a distraction dressed like this," I whispered in her ear.

She snorted a laugh. "If you look around, those boys aren't the only ones staring, deary."

A quick scan of the crowd confirmed what she said. I took my seat, trying to disappear into the crowd, but Gypsy had made that impossible with this dress and the hair and makeup job. Unfortunately, I stuck out like a diamond in the center of a pile of coal.

The whistle sounded, and everyone settled in their seats. Jaden and his groomsmen stepped to the altar. When they turned to look at the procession, all eyes turned to the back, except mine. Our gazes met, and for a moment I saw a flash of the pain mirrored in my heart. It should be me walking down the aisle, not that bitch Eleanor.

I wanted to tell him not to worry, that this would be very short lived. Instead, I gave him a small smile of commiseration. When the music shifted, I turned away and watched the bride appear.

She looked almost transparent all dressed in white. Whoever had done her makeup had made her look like a truly deranged fairy. I had to look down at the ground to stifle a laugh. Brides are supposed to be beautiful, but somehow Eleanor missed the mark. The dress was stunning, but it probably looked better on the store display than on her.

I glanced at Jaden. The flash of disdain was brief, but I caught it when his gaze jumped away from Eleanor to me. I pressed my lips together against an amused smile. His dimples appeared for a moment at the shared inside joke, but with it came deep despair. He looked away, focusing on his wife-to-be as she finished her walk up the aisle.

The words didn't compute as I watched the exchange of vows and rings. My hands fidgeted, and I found myself twirling the ring on my finger, feeling the metal under my fingertips, assuring myself that his heart was indeed mine despite this farce.

"I now pronounce you husband and wife," the high priest announced. "You may kiss your bride," he added as everyone started clapping.

They leaned in, pressing their lips together in an awkward kiss. It held no passion or any sort of affection. They parted and looked out at the crowd with equally awkward smiles. The music started, and Jaden went to take her hand and lead her down the aisle towards the reception hall.

Eleanor's eyes bulged, and her hand flew to her throat. It started at the point of contact. Her lips turned grey, crumbling in the soft breeze. No sound escaped, but someone in the audience screamed. Jaden took a horrified step away as her fingers turned to dust.

My curse was potent and deadly far beyond my expectations. Enough so that I wondered just how badly the backlash would be. Within moments, Eleanor was nothing but ash swirling in a small cyclone of air.

Most of the front rows dispersed, but Samantha stood staring at the death of her replacement. The horror in her profile matched that of most of the audience.

Her gaze snapped to Jaden's, and her face transformed into a mask of fury to the point I swear daggers were going to literally shoot from her eyes and impale him to the nearest tree. Her rage was as palpable as a coming storm.

"What have you done?" she snarled.

He shrugged and shook his head, unable to answer her because he had no idea what just happened. I was the only one in sector eleven who knew.

"What. Have. You. Done?" Her shrill voice blanketed the crowd, and everyone watched as the Regent began to shake with the anger coursing through her.

Dread filled ever fiber of my being. I didn't think trying to save Jaden from a life of servitude would put him in Samantha's crosshairs. But I was clearly shortsighted from the looks of the wrath pulsing from inside her, filling her face with an unnatural red hue.

"Warlock!" she shrieked and pointed at him.

The accusation hung on the air, freezing everyone in place. With that word came a litany of horrors. I had seen the beaten, broken men led to their deaths. I had seen the results of being labeled a warlock. Trial and exile were the civilized parts. I cringed when the guards grabbed him.

Samantha Mallory had just sentenced her only remaining son to death with that one word.

His gaze widened and he shook his head, but before he could speak, the guards hauled him away.

"I didn't do anything!" he cried just before he disappeared into the mansion.

This was not what I expected. I knew what came next. My entire form shook. I caught his gaze just before he disappeared. He didn't reveal me in the crowd, but from the sadness in his eyes, he had to know I was the one to cast the spell.

I was the one to damn him.

Gypsy laughed under her breath. I glanced at the utter joy painted on her face, then turned and walked out of the area, weaving through the crowd until I was standing out in the middle of the street. My breath pulled in harsh pants. This was the backlash to my spell. This was karma in action. My protection spell cursed Jaden. I walked him right into a death sentence.

Panic filtered into my cells. I turned towards the estate. Gypsy grabbed me by the arm with the biggest grin on her lips and guided me back towards her shop. I let her lead me while she cackled and rejoiced at the end of Samantha's bloodline.

Chapter 16

By the time Gypsy led me into the thrift shop, I was numb from both the cold and the events of the last week. Everything I did had backfired. My potion may have saved him from a life of slavery, but it also sentenced the man I loved to death.

"I can't wait to see that witch's face when her son is torn to pieces by the ravagers."

Gypsy's words finally penetrated my mind. "You really believe that is a just punishment?" I snapped.

Her gaze narrowed. "He violated the law."

I let out a high-pitched laugh. "You know as well as I do what a farce the male witch law is."

Gypsy pressed her lips together in a thin line. "He used magic to kill."

My laugh died in my throat as I realized the mistake I had made. "And what if it wasn't him that cast the spell? What if it was a protection spell gone awry?"

"It doesn't matter. Intent matters. If the spell was cast to protect, that is one thing. If it was cast specifically to kill, then it was dark. As dark as Samantha."

I shifted and shivered. "I forgot your coat." I turned to go retrieve it. I needed time alone with my thoughts.

"I'll go with you," she said.

I put my hand up. "I need some time to really digest what happened today. I guess I just never knew he had any abilities. I lived under their roof for years..." Up to a week ago, that was an accurate statement, but with how much Gypsy hated the Regent, and Jaden by default, I didn't think lying was out of line. After all, if I spilled the truth, I might find myself marched right into Samantha's clutches. Prudence outweighed the need for honesty in this new and fragile friendship. "I shouldn't be long."

I let the cold air penetrate my bare shoulders as I headed back. Halfway there, my feet were screaming. For someone so new to high heels, the least I should have done was change my shoes before making this trek.

The pain in my feet and the cold accosting me seemed like the perfect brew to study my underlying reasons for casting the spell. I loved the man, and as much as I hated to admit it, the thought of him being with another woman like he had been with me the other night really crawled under my skin. But I had no inkling of how making love to him felt when I'd spun the spell.

I just wanted my best friend to be happy. I didn't want him to become a slave to his new wife or worse. If she ever found out about his abilities, unless she loved him, he would be exiled.

My intentions were pure when I mixed the spell. If it had been after I had the run in with Eleanor, my intentions wouldn't have been so pure. I sighed as I approached the estate and the crowd that hadn't dispersed yet.

I slipped around pockets of people, hearing snippets of conversation, most of which centered around the shock of the entire wedding events. Instead of eavesdropping, I slipped through the gate.

"I forgot my coat," I said and pointed towards the garden.

"The coats are in the atrium of the mansion," the guard said and pointed up the stairwell.

I gave him a tight smile and climbed the stairs. I had no idea there would be access to the inside of the estate. My mind began to race, focusing on how I could get to where they held Jaden.

Bartrum, a kindly butler stood near the coats. I approached, pulling out the ticket I had been given. He matched it up and handed me my coat.

"May I use the facilities?" I asked, feeling my face turn red at having to ask a man for permission to use a restroom.

He glanced around then gave me a nod. "They are down that hall," he said and pointed towards the executive hallway I had gone down earlier this week.

"Thank you, sir," I said, catching myself before I uttered his name.

The dungeons were accessible from the executive wing. If he had sent me towards the residential wing, I would have been completely out of luck.

I stopped in the ladies' room and hung the coat inside the bathroom stall. I slid the sandals off, positioning them far enough back in the stall so a glimpse could be had if someone was looking for occupied stalls. I locked the door and crawled under the opening, thankful that the floors had already been scrubbed.

I checked the hallway and gathered up the length of my dress, bolting towards Samantha's office. The light was on inside, so I tiptoed past the door. I snuck by, praying my protection spell would keep me invisible to her, then reached the elevator without notice.

Holding my breath, I punched the last sequence I had seen a guard use when I was cleaning the floors the week all hell broke loose. Nothing happened. I closed my eyes, cursing the security of this place. The swish of the doors snapped my eyes open, and I exhaled and stepped inside the lift, silently thanking the gods for their timing. The guards hadn't changed the code yet. I stared at the options after the door closed. I didn't know which level to choose at first, then logic seeped in under the numbness and I hit the button for the lowest level, the level for the most heinous of offenders.

My heart pounded. I had never ventured into the dungeons because it wasn't a place Jaden was willing to go explore. He always wanted to be far away from the complex and anything to do with the criminals locked within the cells down here. When the door opened again, I understood why.

Dark halls met my gaze. I considered conjuring a light spell but thought against it. The cold from the smooth concrete wrapped around my feet. The hall was lined by bars on both sides.

Each step was more uncomfortable than the next. The first few cells were empty, and I began to wonder if I had chosen the wrong floor. The next cell wasn't empty, but I couldn't see who was in the shadows.

I stepped close to the bars. "Jaden?" I whispered.

My breath caught in my throat when the thing turned. I barely got out of reach before the caged ravager swiped his clawed hand through the air, grabbing for me. The gray form bared his razor sharp teeth at me, hissing. Thinking this thing, this cement-colored monster, was once human sent a chill from the base of my spine all the way to my cranium, and I took another step away. Claws scraped across my back. I spun to another beast in the cell behind me. Horror filled me and I stumbled the way I came as the growling noises reached a frenzied pitch.

I pounded the button. When the lift doors opened, I jumped in and pushed the button for the next floor. My heart slammed in my chest, and my harsh gasps didn't help. What the hell was Samantha doing with caged ravagers?

The doors opened to the next floor, which was different than the lowest level. This one at least had more lighting and the floor wasn't as cold. I was still freaked from the face-to-face with the death machines below, so I proceeded with caution. All my mother's warnings now made much more sense.

Each empty cell I passed set my nerves on edge. Halfway down the hall, I halted with a gasp.

Jaden looked up from the chains holding him to the far wall in an open space that I could only deduce was used for the particular brand of torture afforded to warlocks. His shirt hung in tatters, and his bare chest was marred with bruises. So was his face. He blinked slowly, like he didn't believe I was real.

"Star?"

I took a step towards him.

My movement seemed to slap the grogginess from him and replaced it with raw fear. "You can't be here," he whispered.

"Jaden." I moved closer, my heart hurting with the sight of him beaten and bruised. "I'm sorry. All I meant to do was protect you."

His sad eyes didn't match the soft smile he sent me. "I know, but if my mother finds out, she'll live up to her threats." He coughed and spit a wad of blood on the floor to his side.

"Why did they do this?" I asked, reaching for him. My fingers trailed down his chest. He winced when I grazed one of his bruises.

"Because this is what they do to warlocks. You've seen enough exiles to know the condition of the poor bastards when they are banished."

I met his gaze, and my hand fell from his skin. The burn of anger filled me. "You are not the one that should be locked up. I am the one that put the spell on you."

"Why would you do that?" he asked, tilting his head to study me.

"Because you deserve to be happy and not a slave to someone's every whim."

He laughed under his breath, and some of the humor returned to his green eyes. "You still think that, even after the shit I've been?"

"Yes. I never wanted to see you locked into a loveless marriage and a slave to someone so filled with hate," I said. "And I certainly never wished you dead."

"A lot of people in this sector think I did that horrific thing. Did you know that would happen?"

My gaze dropped to the floor. "If the intention of your bride is not pure, then at the kiss announcing man and wife, your bride turns to dust." I gave him a shrug. "That's the spell, so I can't exactly say I didn't know what would happen when I cast it. I guess I just hoped the witch that was ultimately picked really did love you, or at least had pure intent. But after the heinous things Eleanor said to me at the bridal salon, that hope was dashed. I didn't think it would be so...so spectacular." I met his gaze. "She hated you, Jaden."

"A lot of people in sector eleven hate me."

His brutal honesty shocked me. I only knew the boy I played with and raced with. The boy whose warmth and laughter had filled every moment away from the estate. "How can that be?"

"I am at my best when I'm with you. I'm more like that bastard in the street that let those dogs attack you when I'm not."

I stepped away from him. I was aware of the line of women who he dated and dumped, but I just suspected they weren't right for him. I didn't think he was capable of being a dick.

Apparently, I was wrong.

I thought back to the night I eavesdropped on him and his mother. I had never heard venom in his voice before that night, but if that was his normal persona, who the hell had I known all my life?

"How do you reverse it?" he asked, shocking me out of my thoughts.

"You marry a girl who loves you."

Silence filled the cell, and his eyes closed. "That would be you, and my mother would just assume see us both dead before that happens."

"Did you know she has ravagers in cells on the bottom floor?"

His eyes snapped open, and a crease appeared between his eyebrows. My question made the chains holding him rattle. "What?"

"I went there by accident and..."

"What the hell were you doing down there?"

My mouth fell open at the sharpness in his tone. "You...knew?"

His mouth opened as if he were going to speak, but then closed it as his eyes cast to the ground. When his gaze found its way back to mine, his eyes pleaded with me. "We're trying to find a cure."

"We?"

"My mother has been trying to find a cure for years." He hadn't answered my question. Instead, he opted to stare back at the floor. "I went to school for molecular genetic pathology, Star."

"So, you trap those beasts and perform tests on them?"

He nodded. "Sort of. We do tests on their blood. But nothing has worked. My mother lost patience with trying to cure them and decided since we couldn't cure them, she would figure out how to control them."

"You can't control a wild beast," I said and crossed my arms. My mother's words of monsters within sunk in, as did the ramifications of Jaden's knowledge. "So, technically, you are responsible for my mother's attack?"

He closed his eyes, and his chin dropped to his chest. "I didn't know my mother was going to test one of her new serums out in the real world. I've always told her it was never a good idea to test outside of a controlled environment for that very reason."

"And she just happened to choose the area where my mother was scheduled to work to do a test?" Samantha set it up so that if something did go wrong, my mother would be the casualty. She just didn't realize her younger son would be out there, too.

"Are you sure it was just an experiment gone wrong?" I asked when he didn't answer.

His gaze met mine, and he sucked in a breath. "No. I'm not sure." Tears filled his eyes. "But I do know she blames me just as much as she blames your mother for Jack's death. Your mother shouldn't have been tutoring him at that time. He wasn't scheduled to be with her in the garden for another hour. Your mother traded tutoring schedules without passing it by Tasha, and I was the one who struck the death blow, just like I did with your mom."

Dumbstruck, I asked, "Why? Why would you kill them if there was the remote possibility of a cure?"

"There is no cure. We've exhausted everything there is between science and magic combined, and nothing works. I made a choice. I didn't want my little brother to become one of those things just so my mother could use him as a test subject. It's cruel." Tears flowed down his face and his lips trembled as the words tumbled out. "If I don't die when she exiles me, that's exactly what I'll become," he whispered. "My mother's test subject."

I huffed a strangled laugh. "I've been your mother's test subject for years. Did you know about that, too?"

He recoiled as much as the chains would allow. The horror painted on his face told me exactly what I needed to know. Jaden had no idea how many experiments his mother made me endure.

"What tests?" he asked in a hoarse whisper.

"New magic meant to harm. I survived, but it wasn't without pain. I don't think everyone she experimented on fared quite as well."

The sadness in his eyes transitioned to a fiery anger. He struggled against the chains before falling back in exhaustion. "I told her that if she ever laid a finger on you, I would quit. I would walk out of here, and she wouldn't have a prayer finding either a cure or another witch to help her keep the ravagers out of sector eleven without me. Goddamn manipulative bitch," he snarled.

"She was hurting you while she held your safety over my head?"

"Why should I believe you?" The question left my mouth without permission. There was so much I didn't know about this man. He had a long list of secrets and I had no idea just how deep they went.

Jaden's gaze softened. "I've never lied to you, Star. Ever. I just didn't tell you what kind of science I actually studied or what I've been doing with my degree."

I held up my left hand to show him my ring. "So, what's with this? If you knew it was impossible, why even try?"

"Because when I got out of school, I thought I could change the world, and that included marrying who I was in love with, and not marrying for a damn legacy that I don't believe in." He let out a sarcastic laugh. "I guess I was never meant to get what I really want." He closed his eyes again. "You need to go. If she finds you here, even in that disguise, she'll know it's you."

"So?"

He slowly focused on me again. "She will kill you just to spite me."

I took a deep breath. "So, I'm just supposed to watch you be exiled and attacked by those beasts?"

"Yes. That's exactly what you're going to do."

"Bullshit." I stepped so close, I could feel his body heat. "I cannot stand by and watch you be exiled for something I did."

"Don't be a hero, Star. Just go. I can deal with anything that happens to me if I know you're safe." He stared into my eyes. "Please, just do this for me."

I hung my head, resting my forehead on his shoulder. The contact of my skin against his sent a jolt through me, and my hands found his waist, gently caressing his sides for a moment. He let out a soft groan as I leaned against him.

"I love you, Jaden," I whispered and pressed my lips to the side of his neck.

I turned and walked out of the room. He was right about one thing—if his mother found me, I'd probably be thrown into one of the other cells until we both were exiled into the land of the ravagers.

Chapter 17

After retrieving my heels and Gypsy's coat from the bathroom, I finally stepped into the hallway. I didn't bother looking where I was going and nearly ran into Samantha coming down the hall like a hurricane.

"What the hell are you doing in here?" she snapped.

I pointed towards the ladies' room, eyes wide. "I forgot my coat and needed to use the facilities, ma'am." My nerves were already frayed, but I had the presence of mind to keep in character. I needed to move, to get out before she took a closer look at me. "I'm sorry," I added and resumed my hasty exit.

"Your aunt must be ecstatic with how events unfolded," she snarled after a few paces.

Her words created a tremble in my muscles, and I slowed to a stop. "I don't share my aunt's enthusiasm," I said without looking back.

I was through the gate and away from the crowds when the skies opened up. The bitter rain pelted me, washing away all traces of the rainbow of colors in my hair and the glamour Gypsy had set in place. By the time I stepped inside the door of the thrift shop, I was shivering and back to my old self.

A train of wet fabric trailed behind me as I crossed the store to the door of the apartment. I wasn't sure whether to knock or just enter. I did both at the same time.

Gypsy looked up at me with such a glare I nearly slammed the door closed and took flight until my gaze dropped to the smoky glass globe in front of her.

"You...and that boy?" she growled as if Jaden was toxic, and perhaps he was, but my heart wouldn't pay notice.

I bit my lip and nodded. "Yes. He traded his freedom for mine. He agreed to marry whoever his mother picked if she would release me."

She huffed a laugh. "And you believed him?"

"Yes. I heard him with my own ears," I said, and my hands found my hips. I wasn't going to let this bitter and angry woman tarnish what Jaden did. He might very well be the prick she thought he was, but he had never been that way with me. "Jaden has never once lied to me."

"And yet, he literally threw you to the wolves. He has made it so you can never be seen in public without the magical ruse I fit you with."

I didn't have a response for that. She was right. Both he and his mother branded me an outcast. That wouldn't change with Jaden's exile. I closed the door and leaned on it, staring at the ceiling above me. It took me a moment to collect my thoughts.

"He is far from perfect, but he's perfect for me." I caught her glare and continued. "He's been my best friend..." I let out a little laugh. "My only true friend, actually, since as far back as I can remember, although I didn't know he had abilities until last week."

"So he *is* a warlock," she said, crossing her arms.

I laughed at the tag and shook my head. "No. Not in the sense you're talking about. He has no mastery of the elements. He has only cast one spell that I'm aware of, and that was a truth spell that went awry." I didn't want to get into the fact he didn't necessarily need potions or spells to cast his magic.

Her head cocked.

"He wanted to know how I felt about him, and in delivering the truth spell to me, it affected him as well." I offered a hint of a smile. "He was about as pleased to answer my questions as I was to answer his," I said and my smile faded. "That happened to be the night my mother died." The timing rubbed me wrong and I paused, hating myself for questioning his motives.

She crossed her arms and leaned back in her chair. "That's all well and good, but he murdered that girl. You don't think he should pay for that type of black magic?"

"He didn't cast that spell," I said, meeting her gaze.

She laughed at me. "I didn't realize you were that naïve."

"*I* cast that spell. I was trying to protect Jaden!" I yelled and Gypsy's eyes widened. The burn of frustration surrounded me, and the air became charged. "I'm the one who should be beaten and in chains, not him!" My legs gave out at the weight of my words, and I slid down the door. Tears blurred my vision. "I did this." I dropped my head into my hands.

"Child." Gypsy's soft voice cut through my sobs. Her hand caressed the top of my head until I looked up. She crouched before me with such a sad look in her eyes. "Why?" This time the question was asked with a soft sincerity.

"I cast the spell after I found out he had magic in his blood." I sniffled and wiped my cheeks. "If the witch he married didn't love him, he would be her slave for life, or worse, exiled the moment he slipped and showed his abilities. I've lived that for twenty-two years. I know what a nightmare that is, and I cast a spell to protect him from that kind of pain."

She combed my wet hair away from my face. I didn't know how to read the look she gave as she studied me. "You possess the skills to wield such a binding spell?"

I stared into her eyes and nodded. "I mixed a potion based on an ancient protection spell. I was naive enough when I created it to think perhaps there was some pure intent out there, and perhaps Jaden would be lucky enough to find it. Unfortunately, the moment I ran into

Eleanor in the bridal shop, I knew her wedding day would be short lived."

"And by that time, you were already branded an outcast."

"Yes, but it wouldn't have mattered. I can't reverse what I set in motion. The only thing that will break the spell is for Jaden to marry someone who loves him." I shrugged. "Besides, I really don't regret the outcome. Sector eleven is a better place without the likes of Eleanor in it. She would have been a far worse ruler than Samantha."

She chuckled under her breath. "I can't disagree with you there. But this new fact puts our arrangement at risk," she said, her expression sobering.

I stiffened and gave her a nod. "Can I at least take a hot shower before I go?"

She stood and yielded to the side as I climbed to my feet.

"When you get out, we can have a little chat before I make any sort of decision."

I headed into the tiny bathroom and peeled off the soaked dress. The hot shower felt like a dream against my chilled form, but there was no comfort in the warmth. My mind kept turning over the conversations I'd had with Jaden since he made the mistake of revealing his powers.

The secrets he'd shared were not the kind of secrets I expected. None of them, including the revelation of his intent to propose when I was eighteen. I glanced at the ring on my finger again, just to be sure. It shined under the sheen of water. I sighed before running my fingers through my clean hair.

I wondered just how much of it all was real and how much was a ruse.

Doubting Jaden was a strange and unwelcomed feeling. Regardless of my inner turmoil, however, I couldn't let him take blame for my spell. With that thought firmly in place, I shut off the water and wrapped myself in a plush towel. The discarded dress was gone, and in its place was a pair of jeans and a sweater along with my repaired boots.

I slipped on the clothing and stepped into the heart of the apartment. "Thank you."

She patted the chair at the table next to her, and I crossed and sat where she directed.

"You can't save the boy," she said.

I raised an eyebrow, and she pointed to the crystal ball in front of us. A hazy vision of Jaden beyond the barrier came into focus. Ravagers surrounded him, toying with him in a way that made the fire in me burn. A claw struck his shoulder, and his blood spilled. I batted the crystal across the room, and it smashed into tiny shards.

I glared at Gypsy. "That is only a possible future," I growled. "A crystal ball can only show what has occurred in the past. It cannot predict the future with certainty."

Gypsy was still staring at the mess I had made, but finally her gaze snapped in my direction. She stood, towering over me, and I hopped to my feet, meeting her nose to nose.

"How dare you..." she started.

"No. How dare you! That's what you want to happen," I said, pointing at the remnants on the floor. "That would mean the end of the Mallory bloodline. Isn't that your real hope here?"

She recoiled, her narrowed eyes widening at my blatant accusation.

"If I save him, your hopes of seeing Samantha's bloodline crushed are gone." The swell of anger crested as I outlined her intentions. "I'm not blind. I'm not naive, and I certainly can sense ill intentions. You don't want me to interfere with the exile, do you?"

Gypsy's gaze jumped from mine to the broken orb and back. "No. I don't." She straightened her back, glaring at me. "I want that family destroyed."

I pressed my lips together, and my hands formed tight fists. "You are willing to see an innocent man charged for a crime he didn't commit?"

"It's a means to an end, and I can't let you interfere."

I stepped away, studying her for a moment. "You are just as bad as Samantha Mallory."

Gypsy stumbled back, falling into the seat. I guessed those words were more effective than a slap across the face would have been.

"I will find a way to pay you back for your kindness, but I think my welcome here has just worn out." I turned, crossed over the broken shards, and reached for the doorknob.

The minute I pulled the door open, I knew I was screwed. Six palace guards stood waiting on the other side.

I immediately reacted, darting straight towards them, catching them off guard. I slid right between two of the guards, right under a rack of clothing. It tipped as I moved into another rack. I was out the door before they realized what had happened and a block away before they even stepped outside.

I muttered my protection spell, the one I used a million times over the years to remain unnoticed. Before I reached the edge of the city, a sting in my thigh crippled me, and I fell to the ground, rolling to a stop.

"He said you'd run this way." A guard stepped out of the shadows, holstering his tranquilizer gun.

"Who?" I asked, glancing at the barb in my thigh as the drugs spread though my body, sapping all my strength.

"Your traitor of a boyfriend," he said.

Then all went black.

Chapter 18

My head pounded. I rolled into a ball, covering my ears from the high-pitched buzz filling the space around me. Awareness seeped in, and I rolled on the small hard cot. Cold metal pressed against my lower back. I blinked my eyes open, squinting under the harsh lights.

Blinding pain shut my eyes. I buried my head in the crook of my arm for a minute. When labored breathing filtered over the pounding in my head, I tried to view my surroundings again.

The cell came into focus, and I dropped my head in defeat. I was in the jail at the palace, and there was no way in hell I'd be able to save Jaden from behind bars.

"Star?"

Jaden's raspy voice penetrated my brain. I moaned, curling tighter. I didn't want to talk to him. I didn't want to acknowledge my failure.

"Wake your ass up," he hissed.

I opened my eyes and sent a glare in the direction of his voice. Jaden looked worse than when I left him, but it wasn't because of my blurry vision. Even in his injured condition, relief painted his features when our gazes locked.

"I didn't think you would ever wake up."

Every muscle in my body hurt, but I pushed myself into a sitting position. Irritation layered over my senses as the last words of the guard surfaced in my memory.

"Why would you tell them where I would run?" I asked, but the words sounded more like I had a mouth full of cotton balls than my usual clipped tone.

"I didn't want to." His gaze dropped to the ground. "My mother plied me with truth serum, and I tried to resist. When she didn't get anything from me, she resorted to having the guards beat the shit out of me, and I couldn't hold my tongue anymore."

Agony pulled at the edges of his lips as his attempt at an apologetic smile failed. He lifted a shoulder in a half-assed shrug and winced. The bruises across his chest along with the dark circles around his eyes snapped me from my own misery.

"I'm sorry," he said and lifted his gaze. "She knows I slept with you and made me tell her where you would run to." Tears shined in his eyes.

A lump formed in my throat. When he didn't continue, I tilted my head, wondering about how much he truly revealed.

"She wasn't happy," he added with a huff of a laugh.

"That's all you told her?" I asked.

He nodded. "She already knew I was in love with you."

"So..."

He sighed and shook his head. "I told her it was you down here. Not that woman's niece like she thought."

"That woman wants you dead," I said.

His eyebrows rose. "Well, in a few days, she'll get her wish."

"It's not going to happen." My voice was as strong as my resolve, despite the sadness in his eyes.

His gaze moved from me to a point behind me and then back. I turned and a chill bit at my skin. A gate in the far wall opened to darkness. I moved back into the bars, hugging my legs to my chest. The animal noises coming from that dark hole set every hair on my body on edge.

"Yeah," he said, and a tear slowly tracked down his cheek. "Um. I'm told I get to witness what happens when starving ravagers are let loose."

The chains holding him started to shake. His chin dropped to his chest.

I turned back to the opening, pinpointing that high-pitched squeal. It was the caged ravagers a floor below working themselves into a frenzy as our scents drifted into their snouts.

The click of heels against tile pulled my attention away from the gate. Samantha came into view. The harsh glare she sent toward me made me want to crawl out of my own skin, but at the same time sparked the rebel inside me. I glared back instead of cowering.

"Gypsy Rose has been executed."

I blinked, shrinking back into myself, the rebel inside stumbling. A woman was dead because she helped me. The horrifying truth hit like a sucker punch. I knew it shouldn't surprise me, but it still shook me to the core.

I had no idea how empty Samantha was, how completely pathological and psychotic. I wondered what made her so devoid of true emotion or compassion. Was she born like this or did something so horrific happen to her that it stripped her humanity?

Pity layered over every cell, creating an uncomfortable tingle.

"You really have no heart," I said.

She gave me a ghost of a smile. "You can thank your father for that."

The mention of my dad set my stalled anger ablaze. "Bullshit. The way I heard it, you were an ice queen long before you propositioned my dad."

"You are not as meek as you seem, are you?"

I glanced at Jaden. "My mother didn't think I would survive if you knew how smart I really was."

She let out a dark chuckle. "She was right." She stopped in front of my cell and crossed her arms. "How long did you know about my son?"

The tendrils of her truth spell wrapped around me, but unlike Jaden's which had been ingested, this one just brushed the surface without penetrating. I blinked, faking the symptoms of others I had seen under this particular spell, and stuttered. "I, I, uh, I didn't know until you accused him at the wedding."

She raised an eyebrow. "Are you trying to tell me that in all the years you two have been fuck buddies, you had no idea he harbored the evil warlock gene?"

I laughed in her face, ignoring the vulgar reference. "Evil warlock gene? Where did you come up with that?"

Samantha's gaze narrowed. "Answer me!"

I needed to start acting. Otherwise my ass was toast. "No. I had no idea," I replied in that slightly drugged manner she expected.

"You aren't as smart as you might think."

"Mom, please," Jaden whispered.

Samantha turned and glared at him before she returned her piercing eyes to me. "So, he didn't tell you about the spell that killed his wife?"

I shook my head. "No." Self-preservation rocketed in, stopping my tongue from revealing my culpability. The fact that she was fishing for answers gave me hope. If Gypsy had spilled the truth, I was sure I would already be surrounded by beasts tearing into my flesh with their relentless claws and teeth.

Seeming satisfied with my answer, she faced her son.

"Stand up," she snapped. "It's time for your trial."

"Are you seriously going to go through with this?" I asked.

"He violated the law."

"A farce of a law put in place out of spite!"

"Zip it," she snarled.

I glared at her but kept my mouth shut as four guards marched out of the elevator. Two approached Jaden, and the other two stopped in front of my cell waiting for instruction.

"Make her bleed. I want enough blood to drive those beasts into a murderous frenzy," she ordered. "But I expect that she will be alive and in chains when I return. Understand?"

The soldiers nodded listlessly. They seemed to be under a compliance spell, which didn't bode well for me.

I stepped away from the bars. Whatever horrors they had in store for me, they would not remember their actions, at least not in the light of day. But perhaps their evil would plague their nightmares for years to come.

"Oh, and if you choose to take advantage of the little slut in the meantime, be my guest," she added and sent me a truly evil smile.

"You fucking bitch!" Jaden screamed, but he lacked the strength to fight against the grip on either arm. The guards tasked with hauling him to trial dragged his struggling form away.

Samantha followed without a glance back.

The remaining guards unlocked the gate to my cell. Panic clenched my muscles. I backed into the far gate as they entered, listening for the sound of the elevator doors closing. I shifted my stance, readying myself for a fight I didn't think

I'd win, not with their hungry leers focused on me.

My heart thumped in my chest. The rush of adrenaline sprinted through my blood. The noises from below increased at the smell of my fear. The guards moved to either side of the cell, choosing to come at me from both directions. I glanced around, even up at the ceiling for any usable weapon. My gaze locked on the camera, recording every moment.

I couldn't even fall back on magic. Not with the cameras rolling. If Samantha got wind of my powers before I had a chance to get us out of here, I'd be at the mercy of the ravagers below sooner than she planned.

I still had that one secret left, and now wasn't the time to reveal it.

I knew what these men had in mind. It was apparent in their stalk and the lick of their lips as each one scanned me from head to toe. Not only was I in for a hell of a beating, I was sure if they caught me, I'd end up being their whore for however long they lasted. Just the thought made me shiver. I was sure that was Samantha's hope. To have a juicy and violent video to play for Jaden. Or perhaps once I was in chains, she would make him witness the abuse firsthand.

She wanted him a broken man devoid of fight. My death wouldn't be the thing that tipped that scale. What she was betting on was my beaten and abused form in chains begging for death. Death she would provide in the guise of a mercy killing, but seeing me torn to shreds would strip the last thread of Jaden's sanity.

Jaden was right—his mother was such a vicious bitch.

The guard to my right undid his belt and pulled it out of the loops until he had the buckle in his hand. The end dangled on the floor like a whip.

"You need to be taught a lesson," he said, closing the distance.

The other guard did the same, except instead of holding the metal buckle, his scraped along the floor. His whip was meant to do more than just sting.

He snapped it. The metal bit through the fabric on my jeans, tearing a strip of flesh. I yelped, jumping in the opposite direction and received another lash. I was trapped with nowhere to flee. I threw myself backwards against the bars, trying to escape, trying to force the steel to give.

Another snap connected, this time taking a chunk out of my side. I cried out, pushing harder with my legs as if I could just disappear out of the cage. The creak of metal sparked my first flare of hope. The bars behind me actually gave a fraction. My hope was dashed a moment later with another snap of the belt. I jumped, trying to avoid the bite of metal.

A hand wrapped around my arm. Before I had a moment to compute, my feet were no longer on the ground. I sailed through the air and connected with the metal on the far side of the cell. I collapsed to the floor as my brain screamed, insisting I get to my feet.

They were coming at me, both swinging their belts. But they left a gap between them. I dove into the space, rolling onto my feet back where I started, and slammed my shoulder into the metal bars separating the cell from access to the ravagers below. The metal gave. I landed on the ground just as surprised as the guards behind me.

Before I could scramble to my feet, a hand grabbed my foot and yanked me back into the middle of the cell. I rolled and another strike of the metal buckle tore at my cheek. I focused on the guard dragging me back into the room and kicked. The heel of my boot connected with his knee.

He howled and let go, grabbing his injured leg. I rolled onto my hands and knees, hell-bent on getting through the hole I created when leather wrapped around my neck and tightened.

"You aren't going anywhere," the guard's voice growled as he yanked, bringing me to my knees.

My breath wheezed in and out. My lungs burned as I tried to get some sort of grasp on the leather belt strangling me. Starbursts speckled my vision, leaving me lightheaded.

Pain flared in my cheek as the other belt snapped against my skin.

"She said she wants her alive," the guard approaching me said, unrolling the belt from his hand.

The noose around my neck loosened enough for me to get a grip on the leather and pull far enough to get air. I drew in a deep breath, gasping. The guard who had just whipped my face stepped in front of me, close enough so I had a full view of his hands fumbling with his zipper.

The other guard pulled me against him, his knees digging painfully into my shoulder blades and the back of my head pressed against his already hard member. I had one chance to get away. Otherwise I'd be choking on cock.

I balled my hand into a fist and leaned forward enough to give me a little momentum. Then I threw my head back, and at the same time, I delivered an uppercut with everything I had. Both my head and my fist connected with their groins, exactly where I intended.

Each guard let out a pained "oof."

I had just enough time to yank the end of the belt from the captor behind me and roll to the side before the guard in front of me was able to get his bearings. He grabbed hold of my shirt. Before he could pull me back, the fabric ripped, and I went flying toward my goal.

The race was on. I scrambled through the broken bar into the blackness beyond the cell, clawing at the belt around my neck. I never saw the stairs until I missed the first step and tumbled.

I rolled and landed flat out on the ground. I panted as I unthreaded the noose, slipping it off my throat while I caught my breath. I didn't have time for a full assessment of my condition. All I knew was I didn't break my neck.

Lights filtered from above, and the ravager howls filling the space drowned out everything else. I had to hide, or otherwise this brief reprieve would be just that. Then the real fun would begin. My chest remained tight as if one of the guards' belts had wrapped around it and squeezed until breathing became nearly impossible.

I quickly surveyed the area, and my chest loosened a fraction. There were no visible cameras, giving me a sliver of hope. I scuttled to the side into the shadows and closed my eyes, concentrating.

"I am but a shadow, pay no attention to me. I am but a shadow, so mote it be," I whispered and curled myself into a tight ball in the corner of the stairwell.

The beasts inside their cages continued howling and snarling, but the guards' flashlights passed over me and didn't return.

"Where the hell did she go?"

I kept silently repeating the spell as they passed. The breeze from their pant legs swept my face. I held my breath. The flashlights traveled over all the cells, allowing me a second view of the creatures locked on this level.

Saliva dripped from sharp fangs as they paced in their cages. Their beady red eyes focused on the guards as they passed. I counted four rabid ravagers pacing in their cages like the wild beasts they were. Beyond them at the farthest point from the elevator stood a calm one. Its eyes were different, almost human in shape, but with red irises planted in the middle of a sea of white. While the others hunched over on all fours, this one stood on two legs sniffing the air. When the guards shined the light in on him, he glared at them, baring teeth as sharp as razors.

He stepped towards the bars separating him from the guards. The guards moved backwards, hugging the wall, and even I smelled their fear when the beast wrapped his huge clawed hands around the metal. The glare of his nails caught my attention. They looked like the deadly paws of a black bear, but they were absent of hair.

"Have you seen a girl?" one of the guards asked in a shaky voice.

The ravager licked his lips and smiled. He pointed at the guard and then curled his finger in a silent request to come there. The fool stepped closer. I almost came out of my shadow spell, but common sense stopped me. If I stopped him from stepping into the devil's grip, I would be the focus of the two guards, and Samantha would get exactly what she wanted.

The beast curled his finger again, and the idiot obliged.

"Are you the one who drew her blood?"

I blinked at the fact the beast spoke, but the voice had a gravel quality that reminded me of a talking corpse. I whispered the shadow spell again just to make sure I kept my invisibility intact.

The guard let out a small laugh. "Not as much as I would have liked."

The beast's hand lashed out. Its nails pierced the poor bastard's throat straight through.

The ravagers reached a frenzy at the smell of fresh blood. They paced and howled and threw themselves against the bars trying to get to the dying guard.

The second guard's flashlight fell from his hand, and he bolted past me up the stairs. His footsteps along with the animals' howling, almost drowned out the beast's next words.

"That is my blood you spilled," he growled and shook the body at the end of his claw.

With one gone and the other twitching, I stepped out of the darkness, careful to avoid coming within reach of the cells. The light spun on the floor in slow motion, and each step felt dreamlike as I approached the cage. I had no idea where I was going, but I knew going back upstairs was just as much of a death sentence as getting within reach of these creatures.

The advanced ravager's claws retracted, and he tossed the body within reach of the cages next to him before his sharp eyes focused on me. I ignored the sound of ripping flesh and snapping bone, stepping beyond the spectacle to stand in front of the caged anomaly.

"Starlight, star bright..." he whispered and sniffed the air. His eyes closed, and his hands again wrapped around the bars. "First star I see tonight."

"Wish I may, wish I might, have this wish I wish tonight," I finished the phrase.

His eyes opened. A trace of humanity showed itself in the flare of pain in his eyes.

"You smell like your mother," he said.

I stepped back against the cold wall. "My mother is dead."

His forehead dipped against the bars. He was so human-like. I paused, watching the others share with those that couldn't reach the hot meal. That simple act told me more about these beasts than I had learned in all my twenty-two years.

They not only toyed with their victims, but they took care of their pack. I glanced back at the man-thing.

"Why can you speak?"

His soft chuckle sent a chill through me.

"We all speak, but I've been cursed by the Regent, so both man and beast can understand me." His gaze rose to the ceiling, and his claws tightened in time with the muscles in his jaw. "She's the one that made me into this thing. Her magic left me in this between realm."

"Between?"

"Somewhere between a beast ruled by bloodlust and an intelligent being. It makes me more cunning and dangerous than my kin. One bite and I turn my victims, sentencing them to this hell."

He turned and looked at the others in the cages next to him. "They have to nearly kill their victims to turn them into a savage beast."

I thought I heard envy in the gravel-like voice. When his gaze returned to mine, I swallowed hard. Something deep inside made me step closer to the bars.

He put his hand up, stopping me. "Don't. Please."

Despite the alarms clanging in my head, I stepped within reach. "Who are you?" The question came out in barely a whisper, although the thunder of my own heartbeat almost made the question silent in my ears.

He just stared at me and cocked his head to the side. His hand reached out, and the soft pad of his thumb grazed the cut on my cheek. He stepped back, putting distance between us as he licked my blood off his finger.

"You already know," he said and took another step away. "Now, please go before the beast takes over."

His form shook, and his eyes flooded red. When he launched at the bars, I jumped out of reach.

"Run, baby girl," he said and gnashed his teeth in a predatory growl. He pointed away from the dark stairwell.

I scooped up the discarded flashlight and followed his direction, wondering if I was running to freedom, or into another horrific trap.

STAR CROSSED

Chapter 19

I walked through the dark maze of caves, manmade stairs, and finally mud hallways until I reached a wall. I scanned every inch of the dirt with the flashlight.

Nothing.

A dead end.

I turned and leaned on the hard-packed wall with the flashlight pointing at the ground, cursing my gullibility. I stared into the blackness, finally letting all the questions and doubts in. I sunk to the ground, burying my face in my hands. Hot tears stung as they ran through the cut on my face.

That thing in the cell... That thing was my father. The fact that he had been locked up for the last twenty-two odd years burned, and my mother's half-assed warnings finally started to make sense. Had she known about him when she was alive?

"Mama, did you know?" I asked the dark.

No answer came. When I dropped the light, a flash in the corner near the floor caught my attention. I ran my hand across the space until it caught on a hinge. I traced back until I felt an edge and pried the panel open, revealing a green and red button. I picked up the flashlight, and with my heart jumping, I pressed the green button.

The wall trembled and slowly rose. I waited until it stopped and peered out into Samantha's gardens. My teeth clenched as I pressed the red button, testing it out before taking any action. The wall came down fast. Faster than I had time to react. The thought of being crushed to death by a slab of rock wasn't appealing, but if I left the gate open and Samantha let those beasts loose, then I would be endangering the entire sector.

I closed my eyes and shuffled through the catalog of spells I had read, silently thanking the gods for my photographic memory. I considered a force spell, but I wasn't sure what that would do. What I really needed was to have more time to get through the opening. I opened my eyes and pushed the green button again, opening the gate.

As soon as it was up, I said, "Time, I order you to stand still. No minutes pass until I'm safely through this gate. Time stand still, I order you."

I punched the red button and closed the panel, rolling under the wall as it slowly descended. The minute my body cleared the path, the heavy rock slammed down. I took a deep breath of clean air and stared at the darkening sky and the nearly full moon cutting the horizon.

Public exile took place on a full moon, which meant I had twenty-four hours to figure out a plan. I crawled into the heart of Samantha's rose garden and slumped on a bench. I turned the flashlight off and closed my eyes, taking stock of my injuries. I wasn't sure if a rib was broken, but outside of that grinding pain in my midsection, it wasn't as bad as it could have been.

I climbed to my feet and turned toward the western edge of the property. I wouldn't have much time to clear the wall before the alarms would go off. The trial would conclude before the sun set. I needed to get to the safety of our high rise. If not, my opportunity would slip away.

"I am but a shadow, pay no attention to me. I am but a shadow, so mote it be." The mantra fell from my lips as I navigated the garden to the outer wall. Climbing the old tree proved harder than I expected, and I nearly fell as I crawled to the drop point.

I stared down at the ten-foot drop and clenched my teeth in preparation for the pain. I had never once done this injured, and even at my best, the fall jarred every bone in my body.

"Suck it up," I whispered into the dark and rolled, grabbing the lower branch to dangle from.

I counted to three and let go. The landing nearly ripped a yelp from my tightly clenched lips. I fell to my knees just as the alarms sounded.

Although I was outside the gate, I was far from safe. I would have to skirt around the buildings to get to the high rise with my safe room. The only question I had was whether Jaden would give up that particular building or not. I limped, repeating the mantra.

When I finally looked up, I was at the edge of the tall structures. My heart throbbed in my throat. The shimmering barrier separating ravager lands from sector eleven was only a few paces into the city.

The Regent must already know I escaped. Why else would she have blocked access to the old iron structures? I didn't even want to think of the alternative, but it surfaced anyway. If this wasn't intentional, then Samantha's magic was failing faster than anyone could have foreseen.

"Shit."

I just stood and stared because without my safe spot, I had no idea where to find shelter. I looked in the direction of Gypsy's thrift shop and bit my lip. That was the only other place I might be able to hide now that Gypsy was dead.

It was a risk, but I couldn't hold the cloaking spell for much longer. I needed a nap to rejuvenate and then some food to replenish my energy if I had any hope to stop Samantha.

The walk nearly did me in. I almost missed the shimmer and stepped though the barrier just outside Gypsy's doorstep.

"Jesus," I muttered and stepped back into the middle of the intersection. The same intersection where Eleanor's dogs had attacked.

With nowhere to go, I turned and took an uncertain step toward the mansion. Every possible safe zone had been taken from me.

A burning anger boiled to the surface. An electrical storm formed overhead, and lightning flashed in time with the throbbing in my temple. I clenched my fists, muttering to the elements, calling on them to give me strength to do what I needed.

A familiar bite clutched my thigh. I glanced down at the dart embedded in my flesh. When I looked up, the guard I ditched stood ten paces away.

"Fuck," I said.

He grinned as if we'd just shared an inside joke. "Oh, I'm going to fuck you up, alright."

I stumbled but caught myself and yanked out the dart. The sky echoed my frustration, and I screamed. With the full force of my fury, I threw the dart at the guard.

A wind gust took it, turning it into a missile that sailed true. The point pierced the guard's eye, running right through until the point stuck out the back of his head. I didn't think he knew what hit him. By the time he hit the ground, life had already left his body.

The knock-out agent in the dart turned my muscles to jelly and I collapsed in the middle of the street.

STAR CROSSED

Chapter 20

Every inch of my body hurt. I opened my eyes to a gray ceiling. In my peripheral vision, chains hung taut. After a blink or two, my focus moved to the shackles biting my wrists. Lifting my head hurt. I inhaled, holding it for a minute before releasing a breath.

My head lolled to the side against my raised arm. The top of my feet scraped the floor, and it took me a few minutes to find my footing. I slipped in a slick puddle directly underneath me.

My back exploded in pain, and I screamed, arching away from whatever the hell had shredded my skin. Hot trails of liquid ran down the back of my legs. My breath locked in my chest when I glanced down. Cold seeped bone deep to the point I never thought I'd be warm ever again.

I stood in a puddle of blood, enough to indicate whoever was causing the agony in my back had been at it for a while. The puddle grew with each drip down my leg. My breath wheezed from my chest. I forced myself to stand, despite the tacky substance oozing through my toes.

At that moment, I wished to god I had stepped through that barrier and into Gypsy's house. At least there I would have had half a chance.

It took a moment to realize my shirt was in tatters and I had no pants on. The slight shiver turned into an all out shake that rattled the chains keeping me bound.

I faced the open cavern with my back to where Jaden was the last time I was imprisoned. An emptiness wrapped around me at the thought of what happened between the time I passed out in the street and now.

"Jaden?" I whispered with a voice laced with death.

He stepped into view holding a bloody cat-o-nine tails in his hand. The smile that drew to his lips chilled me, as did the blood-splatter on his chest and face. Jaden was no longer in control of his actions, or his mind.

He stepped closer, and the fading shimmer of a spell reflected in his eyes.

"Please, Jaden, fight this. *Please*," I begged.

He paused and blinked, and awareness brightened his eyes. The struggle for command over his body revealed itself in both the tightening of his jaw and his fists. Raw fury bloomed in his jade irises, accompanied by bone-crushing agony as he fought against his mother's magic.

"I want her broken," Samantha's voice demanded from behind us.

"Fuck...you," he growled in broken syllables. "I'm not doing this."

A dart whizzed by me and embedded in his chest. He met my gaze with a desperation I didn't fully comprehend until he wobbled on his feet.

"I hate you," he whispered, looking past me at the object of his loathing. Then he collapsed onto his knees in front of me.

Seeing Jaden's ability to fight his mother's spell compromised sent tremors through my form. Without awareness, he wouldn't be able to resist whatever she had in store.

Samantha approached and pulled the dart from his skin before she whispered her control spell in his ear. She gave me an evil smile as she straightened.

"Break her by any means necessary," she said and stepped out of the cell. "I want her begging for death."

Jaden's bowed head slowly lifted. His glazed eyes frightened me just as much as his slack features. No part of the man I loved was awake or in control of his actions. He was Samantha's puppet, and she was hell bent on destroying both of us.

"Jaden?" I whispered, hoping my voice would trigger him out of this trance like it seemed to before.

He stood and reached out, grabbing my shirt. One yank and the already frayed fabric shredded. He threw the ruined garment on the floor, leaving me exposed in only a bra and underwear. The lack of expression or emotion present in his face nearly made me pee myself.

He licked his lips while he studied me like he was contemplating my torture. He stepped close, and my heart turned to a wild beat, dreading the intensity now in his eyes. His clenched fist struck with such force he actually lifted me off the ground, stripping my lungs of oxygen. My stomach throbbed where he'd connected. I had no chance to recover before the second blow slammed home. This time I did scream.

"Jaden, stop!" I cried.

He stepped closer, looking straight through me. His hand wrapped around my throat, squeezing my airway.

"Ja...den." I forced the word out. Black spots layered over my vision, and I fought the need to pass out. "Please."

His grip loosened, but my reprieve lasted only a second before his left fist cracked my ribs. If he continued, I would never be able to fight off a ravager attack, never mind have a prayer of saving him. My brain raced for an answer, for a way to get through to him.

Another punch drew a second scream, and then his free hand pinched my breast before it traveled lower.

"I heard ravagers like eating pussy," he said in such a smooth tone that my heart froze. His hand squeezed me before he stepped behind me.

The rattle of more chains locked my breath in my chest. Cold metal wrapped around my knee and jerked up. Jaden placed the hook into the link above my hands, raising my knee and exposing me further.

"Don't do this," I cried, but that didn't stop him from doing the same with my other leg. The bonds around my wrists dug in with my full weight being supported by the tight metal.

Jaden stepped in front of me, inspecting his handiwork.

"What are you doing?" I gasped, trying to leverage the chains around my knees for support to alleviate the agony in my wrists.

His slow smile sent a shiver through me.

"Breaking you by any means necessary," he said. His voice had zero inflection. He moved the hem of my underwear to the side and stabbed a finger deep within me. He was not gentle, either, and the fact that Samantha was watching was even more humiliating.

"They will rip off your feet first, but then I think they'll go for this, especially if it's dripping with cum. Maybe they'll even fuck you before they kill you," he said as he kept the relentless pace with his fingers. "I think that's a show everyone will want to see."

I had no hands available to push him away. He squeezed my breast hard, pulling a wince from my lips.

"Goddamnit, Jaden, wake up!" I cried but I couldn't pull away, not even when his free hand started to unbutton his pants.

He moved closer. Close enough so our faces almost collided. Jaden was going to rape me, and I wasn't sure I'd be able to recover from that.

"Stop this," I yelled and head-butted him with everything I had.

My forehead collided with his nose, and I heard a satisfying crunch. Stars filled my vision. Jaden stumbled back a few steps. His hands flew to his face to cover the blood gushing from his broken nose. His eyes glazed with tears of pain. When he blinked the tears away, my Jaden was back in control.

"What the..." he started as he stared at his bloody hands. His gaze lifted to mine before traveling down my torso, focusing on the path of bruises now marring my stomach. After his gaze fell on the chains holding my legs wide open, it dropped to his unbuttoned jeans.

Jaden's lips thinned, and he turned a fiery glare in the direction of his mother.

Another dart flew towards him.

"Stop," he commanded in a low, soft tone, and the dart obeyed, halting a fraction of an inch away from his skin. He ripped it out of the air. "You want to see what I'm capable of, Mother?"

Murderous fury painted his features. The chains holding my legs in place shattered. My feet dropped to the ground like lead weights, pulling out a gasp as the impact traveled through my beaten form.

As much as it killed me to stop him from attacking his mother, and doling out some much needed justice, I had to.

"Don't," I whispered, and his gaze turned to me in disbelief. "Killing her isn't the answer."

"Why the fuck not?" he snarled, still clutching the dart as blood flowed freely from his nose. One of his eyes was now red as well, as if he blew a boatload of blood vessels when he annihilated the chains.

"Because without her, there is no barrier," I said. As much as I hated his mother, she still held the key to sector eleven's safety. I couldn't let his momentary anger put everyone's lives at risk.

Jaden's hands slowly dropped to his side, and his face squeezed in defeat. We both knew he didn't have the strength to hold off a horde of ravagers. I certainly had no strength to lend at the moment. I needed a reprieve from the beatings, from the loss of blood and dignity.

I needed more than a moment or two of rest, and so did he.

Another dart hit him, and he looked at it and then back at Samantha.

"Take him back to his cell," she instructed.

A pair of guards passed by, grabbing him before he collapsed. Her footsteps approached and she stood staring at the hole for a moment before she moved her hard gaze to me.

"I think Jaden will be my new guinea pig," she said, crossing her arms. "I'll make sure he survives tonight, and then I'll keep trying to cure him. But you...you'll die here when I open the gates below. Those beasts will tear the flesh from your bones until nothing is left. I imagine they will toy with you a bit first. They seem to like it when their victims scream." She uncrossed her arms. "Especially your father."

I glared at her, at the confirmation she just made, but I didn't speak. I let her leave without comment. The swish of the elevator doors left me in the silence of the cages. Only Jaden's soft breathing broke the quiet. I glanced over my shoulder to where he lay on the concrete, bound by chains once again.

I leaned my head against my arm before the tears started in earnest.

Hope was a fickle bitch, and right now she left me standing in a puddle of blood, battered and broken.

Chapter 21

I jerked and the chains rattled. I had actually dozed, enough to make everything stiff again. My stomach and ribs still throbbed, but I regained my footing, shifting to try to turn but it hurt. My back burned with every shift, and I could only imagine how many bloody welts traversed my skin. I sucked air through my teeth.

Jaden was still lying on the floor, but his eyes were open. I didn't know how long he had been studying his dirty work, but the self-loathing was visible in both his scrunched face and clenched fists. I forced myself to turn as much as possible without dislocating my shoulder.

"Stop looking like you killed someone," I said.

He huffed but didn't speak. Instead his gaze traveled to the shackles holding me in place all the way to the floor and then back to mine. "It looks like that's exactly what I did. The sentence just hasn't been carried out yet."

"Spare me the pity party," I said. "Did you know?"

"Did I know what?" he asked and slowly sat up. The corner of his left eye still looked like it was filled with blood.

"Did you know my father was locked up downstairs?" I wasn't in the mood to dick around.

His eyebrows rose and then fell before knitting together as he tilted his head. The question in his eyes was enough. He *didn't* know, and then the horror of it hit him, drawing a gasp from his lips.

"Frankenstein?" he asked.

My heart squeezed. Jaden and I had found a legible book in one of the old buildings. It was preserved in an airtight cabinet, so we broke into it. We read that book over and over until the pages were ragged. It was an appropriate name, and the fact he used that sad monstrosity to describe my father made my heart ache.

I nodded and he closed his eyes, dropping his head to the ground. "Jesus, Frankenstein is your father?"

"I think your mother is going to send him to kill me."

He let out a near hysterical laugh and looked at me with tears sparkling in his eyes. "That would be the ultimate screw you, and I wouldn't put it past her." He started coughing and winced.

I turned back towards the dark pit below. The noise had gotten so loud, I couldn't imagine lasting long enough to evoke any sort of protection spell once they were let loose. I glance up at the chains.

"Can you get me out of these?"

"I don't know. Mine are magically enhanced. I don't know if my mother bothered to do the same to yours." His eyes narrowed in concentration.

The chain attached to my right arm started vibrating.

"Open," he whispered and it unlatched.

My arm fell like a dead weight, and I let out a groan of combined pain and relief. I turned around so I could see Jaden. Blood leaked out of his left eye, and his gaze was locked on the second shackle. The slight trembling of the metal along with the heavier flow of blood from his eye, and now his nose, set off my internal alarms.

"Stop!" I yelled, startling him. This was obviously taxing him beyond capacity. "You might need some energy to stop the ravagers."

"And then what? I can't come back and I can't keep this up indefinitely, so why not help free you? Why not make sure you live?"

"Because." I stopped myself from revealing my plan, however lame it seemed at the moment. If I voiced it, the camera would pick it up, and then Samantha would know I was a witch.

"Because what, Star?" He sat up and shrugged, holding his hands up, showing me his binds. "I can't break these. Believe me, I've tried.

I'm as good as dead, and I'd really rather bite it than become one of those things." He nodded towards the opening.

"What if we both survive?"

He wiped his face on his arm and then leaned back against the wall. "What if?"

I nodded. I needed to hear his what-if scenario. I needed some level of calm because my heart had upticked a few minutes ago, like an alarm clock in my soul had gone off and we had run clean out of time.

He smiled and looked up at the ceiling. "What if." His gaze dropped to mine. "I'd marry you." The light laugh that escaped made me smile, along with the distant longing in his eyes. "Actually the first thing I would do is make love to you right and proper. Not that rushed desperate excuse I attempted the other night."

"It wasn't that bad," I said. To me it had been a slice of heaven, but what did I know? He was my first. My only, and all I wanted was for another chance to lie in his arms.

The smile that surfaced on his lips conveyed all sorts of naughty promises. "Honey, I can do so much better than that."

My face heated, and I looked away.

"Our wedding wouldn't be a production like the one Eleanor insisted on. It would be you and me, either on a beach on the south shore or up on the top of a mountain, with only the heavens and a high priest as a witness."

"I'd like to wear a pretty wedding dress," I said and his dimple appeared for a minute.

I hadn't thought much about what kind of wedding I wanted. All I knew was I had wanted my mother there, but that had been stolen from me. Just the thought sent an ache all the way to the bone. I hadn't had proper time to mourn my mother. And thinking about her not being at my wedding clenched my throat.

"You'd be beautiful in anything...or nothing," he said, nodding at my current condition. "But whatever you wanted, I would make sure you got."

I tried to smile but my lips wouldn't obey, so I pressed them together and looked away. "I wish my mother could see me get married."

He sighed and tilted his head. "I wish she could have been here, too."

"I like the idea of a beach wedding," I added to try to keep the despair at bay, but it circled like a pack of ravagers. "Where would you take me on our honeymoon?"

"To the ritziest hotel in this sector, and I'd pamper the hell out of you."

"How?"

"I'd feed you strawberries and champagne while we soaked in a tub together." His smile was far away, and his eyes almost closed.

I could see the dream forming between us. "Then what?" I asked, finding solace in what his future might hold.

"Then I'd make love to you all night until the sun burned through the sea mist."

Just the thought sent a tingle through me.

"Well, isn't that just special," Samantha said as she strolled down the hall.

Neither one of us heard the elevator. I glared at her, angry at her intrusion on this much needed conversation.

Six guards flanked her, and when she stopped in front of my cell, they continued to Jaden's and roughly hauled him to his feet. My blood still spackled his bare chest, and his feet were equally as bare and blood ridden. The scent of fresh blood would drive the ravagers feral, limiting his chance of survival.

My gaze met his, and the loss of hope in his eyes clenched my stomach so much I had to fight to keep upright. Terror formed in the center of my body. I wanted his dreams. I wanted him, and I did not want either one of our lives to end in such a horrific fashion.

"We have just enough time to see at least one ravager attack."

"Let her go, please?" Jaden pleaded as the guards secured his hands behind his back and yanked him into place for a full viewing of my demise.

"No. You've sentenced her to this fate," she said to Jaden, trying to pin my death on his already damaged soul.

"Bullshit!" I snarled with a tremor in my voice. Despite my attempt at a brave face, I was already shaking. My bladder clenched, sending a few stray drops of piss into my panties.

She pressed a button on a remote in her hand, and the creak of metal sounded in the open entry. Footsteps echoed. I tried to yank my wrist from the cuff, but it wouldn't budge. I tried to hide in the farthest possible corner and traded a pained gaze with Jaden.

I would give up every crazy sick adrenaline rush we shared to wake from this nightmare. I didn't want to die, and I certainly didn't want

Jaden to watch this massacre. Hope had fled, and with it went all sense of self-preservation.

"Please, please let Jaden go. He doesn't deserve to die, not for this. He didn't kill Eleanor... I did. I found a spell book..." The words tumbled from my lips at the same rate the tears blurred my vision.

"Interesting," Samantha said with a hardness that matched my unyielding panic.

When the beast that once was my father stepped into the cell, he sniffed the air, glancing between the chain holding me in place and the group standing outside the cell.

"You chained my offering?" He waved towards me.

"I want her bones picked clean, and sometimes a running victim gets away," Samantha said, sending me a glare.

"Stay the hell away from her," Jaden burst, struggling against the guards' hold.

My father stumbled back as if he had been shoved, but he shook it off. With each step closer, the frenzy in his eyes flared. He came right up to me and took a big sniff.

"Blood and fear. My favorite," he said and then ran a nail down my bound arm, splitting the skin.

Jaden thrashed in earnest, like it was his life on the line and not mine. When he nearly ripped from one of the guard's grip, Samantha pointed the remote once more. Seconds ticked and then the horde of ravagers burst through the opening.

Terror washed over every cell as they came directly for me. Their teeth snapped at the air as saliva dripped from their snouts.

"That should do it," Samantha said and started down the hall towards the elevator.

Jaden bellowed, twisting from the guards' hold. His gaze locked on the remaining shackle. The metal burst outward, narrowly missing my father, but a chunk shot clean through one of the ravager's heads, dropping the beast instantly to the ground.

Before any more could be taken down, the guards dragged him towards the elevator. Neither Jaden nor Samantha had a line of sight into the cage when teeth sank into my calf. The worst kind of pain froze my muscles in place. I screamed.

My father reached down and took the beast by the scruff of his neck. He yanked him off me, sending the animal flying into the far wall. The rest of the pack formed a semicircle around us, but remained at a distance, warily watching my father.

He gnashed his teeth and squeezed his fists tight before unclenching and reaching for me. I flinched back, unsure of whether to be frightened or not. The obedience of the rest of the pack seemed unnatural, but then again, I'd only seen them in the wild outside the walls.

His hand wrapped around my arm, pulling me closer. "Scream again like you are in unimaginable pain," he whispered. When I didn't react, he squeezed my arm, sinking his nails into my flesh.

I let out a choking scream until he covered my mouth and brought me close. He turned his gaze to the unconscious ravager and gave a nod to the pack. Instead of attacking me, they turned on their own, ripping one to shreds so all that resounded in the cell were the growls of the beasts and the tearing of flesh.

"I will kill y—" Jaden's scream was cut off by the closing of the elevator doors.

All that followed was a muffled wail.

I leaned in to my father's chest as the tears flowed. Jaden thought I was the one those beasts were tearing apart. He thought I was dead. I needed to get out, to stop the madness before he willingly let the ravagers outside the barrier kill him.

I knew the routine. I had witnessed similar executions. They always began with the orchestrated public trial asking for any reason why the accused shouldn't be exiled. All pleas would be ignored, no matter how valid. My voice wouldn't be heard. Not in time to stop the guards from catapulting Jaden through the barrier where the beasts would be lined up for their next meal.

I knew that defeated look in Jaden's eyes. I knew he would drop to his knees and let them kill him. I had to stop this. Now.

I pushed away from my father's chest and took a limping step towards the locked door with only one focus.

My father's hand gripped my arm, stopping me.

"You have to let me go. I can't let Jaden be exiled for something I did."

His grip on my arm tightened, and he bared his razor-like teeth. The growl that rolled from his throat gave me a start, but he had yet to attack. The pack was still tearing the meat from the bones of their fallen, and until this moment, they hadn't given me more than a cursory glance. But now they all turned to witness the showdown between father and daughter.

"The reason he's here and being exiled today is because I put a protection spell on him. One that prevented him from being kept in a loveless marriage with a cold-hearted witch."

"I dislike that boy," he said in a tone completely unfamiliar, yet very fatherly and protective.

"I don't have time for this." I pulled out of his grip. "Either kill me, or let me go."

His gaze dropped to my injuries, including the bite on my leg. He pressed his lips together and pulled me close.

My heart leapt into my throat until he whispered, "You will need this." His hands grasped my shoulders, and he dipped his forehead to mine.

On contact of our foreheads, raw energy circled around me. I went rigid under the power passing from him into me. My back and calf flared with a burning itch that only lasted seconds. My aching ribs reset in a symphony of pain followed by relief. I gasped.

Knowledge of the power I possessed seeped in as the magic fused with my cells. All sounds of feeding stopped. My father's hands dropped from my shoulders as he straightened. His eyes flashed feral for a moment before he harnessed his inhumanness back in place.

The rest of the pack focused on us, and they growled as one unit and took a stalking step forward. The itch to take the lead took over, but

I needed answers before I could concentrate on communicating with the rest of the ravagers.

"Samantha knew you harbored this?" I asked.

"She has been trying to strip this from me for the last two decades," he whispered. "While her son's experiments were a futile attempt to cure whatever this disease is, her experiments were aimed to drain the power to control the pack."

"Did Jaden know her true plan?"

My father shook his head. "He always talked about a cure. About how we could get better. He was always a little naive that way."

I would have never categorized Jaden as naive, but as soon as my father said it, it held true. This was just as naive as thinking the two of us could be together while his mother still ruled the sector. It was also as naive as believing Samantha wasn't evil. That slanted truth shattered the moment Jaden found himself in chains and witnessed it firsthand.

"She knew she was losing control of the barrier, didn't she?" I thought Jaden suspected as much, which was probably the reason he stepped up his efforts. "And there is no cure, is there?" I stared at the group of ravagers.

He sighed. "No. And as far as creating more intelligent monsters, Samantha was never able to recreate the same circumstances that led to the way I am with either her magic or her son's scientific experiments. There is no cure for what I am and no cure for these beasts." He waved at the pack behind him.

"Intelligent monsters?"

"Precisely. She wanted an army that she could control." He licked his lips. "Now you need to get away from me before I lose control. There is too much blood in this cell, and it is turning my bloodlust into an uncontrollable beast."

Sweat broke out on his forehead, and saliva bubbled up at the corners of his mouth. He was on the edge, and despite me being his flesh and blood, that would soon be his only singular focus. My flesh and blood.

I took a step away and pointed at the remaining members of my father's pack. "Samantha sent one of those things out to the gardens that day to kill my mother. Didn't she?"

"Yes. Because I would not give her this power, and she couldn't steal it from me," he said and took a predatory step in my direction. "Make sure they know what she did. What she is." The whisper of his voice carried a feral growl despite the soft smile. "And make sure they know what *you* are capable of."

The pack advanced just like he had. I turned to the group, pointing at them.

"Back off!" I snarled, afraid of what might happen if I didn't have full control over them. The pack halted and even took a step back. So did my father.

The beast in my father finally surfaced, making his eyes glow red and his lips peel back from his sharp teeth, but he did not attack. None of them did. My eyes widened. While I now harbored my father's alpha powers, the practical application of controlling the pack stunned me. Once I gave a command, they had to obey. The realization left me dizzy, so I reached out, grabbing one of the bars to steady myself. My gaze darted to my father, and he gave me the slightest of growls.

"You had this while you were human?"

He nodded.

This new dynamic stalled my brain and I blinked, unable to corral my pinging thoughts. In some ways, I understood why Samantha coveted this power. It would make her a goddess in the eyes of the sector, and she wouldn't need Jaden.

The thought of him jolted me back to reality, and my internal alarms sounded. I forced myself to focus on the issue at hand.

Getting out of this godforsaken cell block.

"Think," I muttered to myself and did the unthinkable. I turned my back on the pack, but I didn't care. If I didn't get out of this cell, and out of this building, my hopes of sparing Jaden became less and less certain.

The quickest way out of the building was via the elevator, so that was my target. The only thing between me and the elevator was the damn cell door. I focused on the lock keeping me from reaching my destination.

"What is now locked, let be unlocked."

The click gave me a start. I pushed the gate open but stopped half in and half out of the cell, debating. Leaving them locked up didn't seem right, but if I let them out, what kind of hell was I unleashing on the sector?

If I could control them, perhaps I could lead them to freedom without harm to the people of sector eleven. The responsibility of the alpha fell on me, and somehow I knew that if I didn't protect both the pack and the people, my station would mean shit. The pack would turn on me as fast as they had their downed comrade.

Without looking, I said, "If you want your freedom, follow me."

I left the cell door open, doubting my decision, but I knew if I showed a hint of weakness, I would be ripped apart. My heart charged, even as my feet kept a steady pace. The patter of nails on the floor followed. When I stopped in front of the elevator, my father stepped in the space beside me.

Shock, bitter and tinny, filled my mouth. They hadn't attacked, or even sniffed me for that matter. Every nerve in my body tingled, and if someone yelled boo, I probably would have let out a yelp and jumped as high as the ceiling. The door opened, and I took the biggest gamble of my life. I stepped inside and held the door as the pack filtered into the tight space. Cool soft skin brushed my leg.

I focused on the most important piece of instruction for this fool's journey. "If you attack, I will end you. Understand?" I had no idea if I was capable of following through with the threat, but the creatures nodded. I glanced at each ravager, making eye contact before my gaze landed on my father. "That goes for you, too."

His response was a low chuckle that bordered on a growl.

"If you do what I ask, I will lead you beyond the barrier where you will be free of the tests and spells."

"The Regent will never allow that," my father said.

The pack shifted restlessly.

"The Regent will have no choice. She played her hand, and now I am playing mine." The strength and conviction in my voice wasn't contrived, and the power that lay dormant since birth flared in the center of my being. "Jaden is my primary concern. I do not want him harmed. If I need help protecting him, will you help me?"

They rumbled and shifted, exchanging glances with each other before giving me a nod.

"Then we can deal with the Regent." I met my father's gaze. She was the only one that I might consider allowing him to attack, and based on the darkness that flared in his eyes, I might not have a choice.

"You will not be able to get back through the barrier once you breach it," he said.

"If Jaden is already beyond it, that's where I'm going."

His jaw tightened. "This control. It is only temporary." Concern flared in his eyes.

"What do you mean temporary?" My whisper sounded more like a hiss in the tight space.

"I wasn't able to hold off an attack," he said, and the meaning in his eyes dried all the spit in my mouth. "You may have to choose."

"I choose Jaden."

"And if he is already dead?"

The thought never occurred to me, but I wasn't going to let it cloud my judgment right now. If I harped on it, I would lose my focus and my raw nerve to face Samantha on such a bloody battleground.

I needed my wits. I needed to believe Jaden was alive, because if he wasn't, that would be the end of my rebellion. And the end of sector eleven. The barrier would fall because my last act would be to kill the witch.

I was also sure that if I challenged Samantha and stripped her of her Regent station, the wall would fail. I was the only one who could counteract the breakdown of our barrier. I had read those ancient spell books, and I knew exactly what was needed. The spell required blood, but thankfully not a blood sacrifice.

Like all the other ancient spells found in those books, I had memorized every line, every nuance, and every action. I just hoped like hell the combination of elements and spirits I called on would obey me instead of Samantha Mallory.

Otherwise, we were all doomed.

Chapter 22

The estate was quiet. I stepped out of the elevator, aware of my lack of clothing. I couldn't conceive of marching through the streets in only my underwear and bra, but time was not on my side.

I slowed as we approached Samantha's office and put my hand up, halting the pack. The Regent kept an array of jackets in the closet, so I darted inside. I scanned the collection and grabbed the longest one. The red fur-lined trench coat would not only keep me covered, but it would also keep me warm. I pulled it on as I headed back into the hallway.

My father's nose crinkled, as did the beasts' surrounding me.

"I know, but I can't exactly stroll down Main Street and make a stand in my underwear."

I finished buttoning the jacket and tied the sash as we entered the atrium. The guards paused at the sight of us, their jaws dropped. I had to issue a spell quickly before they got their bearings and went on the attack. I needed to stop everything until I had a chance to make things right.

I cast a protective net around my little posse and bellowed, "Gods of the sun and moon, hear my prayer. Stand behind me and add your might to mine. Give me the power to command time."

The impact of the elements hit like a gale force wind. I braced against the pressure, continuing the spell.

"Time stand still. I order you. No minutes shall pass until I am through doing what I must do. Time stand still, I order you!"

I broke out in a sprint. It took the pack a moment to catch up. I knew it was going to be cold out, but I didn't expect a dusting of snow on the ground. I nearly went tumbling down the stairs. My father's arm wrapped around my waist, picking me up as the pack effortlessly traversed the stairs.

The guard at the gate didn't move. He didn't even look as we passed. I smiled, letting my father carry me as they ran. Their sprint left me breathless at the speed and agility they displayed. When we rounded the last corner, my breath sucked in at the thick crowd frozen in time.

The ravagers dodged through the crowd without stopping. As soon as we entered the executioner's circle, we stopped. My gaze shot to the shimmer of the barrier and the wild ravagers surrounding Jaden in the same horseshoe form as the crowd.

My heart hammered against the walls of my chest. This was the scene Gypsy showed me in her crystal ball. Jaden's wrists were bound behind his back, and he knelt on the ground with his head bowed. His right shoulder had already been torn, but I couldn't tell if it was by teeth or claw. The beast coming in for another attack didn't have blood dripping from his mouth. None of the close attackers had blood on their snouts.

My father put me down and glared at Samantha. I ran straight for Jaden, and the pack followed. The minute I burst through the barrier, time shifted back to normal.

"No!" I screamed as every hair on my body stood on end.

One of my pack launched, catching the attacking ravager before he reached Jaden.

Jaden's head snapped up at the sound of my voice. His tear-filled gaze met mine. Confusion crossed over his features, and his gaze traveled over the pack as it created a barrier between us and the wild ravagers.

"Were you bitten?" I asked. I suspected he wasn't, but I wasn't sure.

"Not yet," he said. "How..."

"Subterfuge. My father faked it."

"Did your father bite you?" he asked, struggling to his feet, his gaze leery as he studied me.

"No." I didn't expand on the fact one of the other ravagers took a bite out of my leg, nor did I tell him my father healed all my ailments. I didn't think he realized how powerful my father was. Behind me, my dad was close to the barrier and using Samantha as a human shield against the advancing guards.

Another ravager launched, and Jaden stumbled closer to me, but my pack stopped it.

"Is this you?" He waved towards our personal safety barrier, his eyes as wide as I'd ever seen them, making his green irises stand out.

"Yes." I offered a shrug. "My father gave me a little gift. Something your mother has been trying to steal from him for years."

His jaw dropped.

"But it won't last," I said.

He blinked like I had short-circuited his brain, and then his eyes hardened. "Jesus, woman, then why the hell did you come out here?"

"For the same reason you just gave up without a fight."

His cheeks turned red, and his gaze fell to the ground. "I thought..."

"I know what you thought," I snapped.

The creatures holding the line started their restless shuffle. I grabbed Jaden and backed towards the barrier. The control was ebbing, and with it our chance of survival.

I glanced over my shoulder. The barrier was an arm's length away. I stepped closer, putting enough distance between Jaden and me. My gaze shifted to my father's dark stare. He smiled in a gleefully evil way.

I shook my head. "Don't you dare," I growled, but my command wasn't strong enough to stop his thirst for revenge.

His teeth buried into Samantha's throat. Then he threw her through the barrier.

I grabbed Jaden and dove as bullets rained through my father. Each shot jerked his body. I pulled Jaden farther away from the kill zone. His mother thrashed on the ground, screaming as the virus fought for control. It would be a blessing if she bled out before it turned her, but with the knowledge my father had given me, I knew better. Once the virus was in your system, that was the end.

The beasts held in captivity turned their attention to their mistress, baring teeth in what looked like an ironic smile.

My father's body fell through the barrier. He reached out, grabbing my ankle as I tried to shuffle us away. The connection of skin against skin shot enough power into my form that I thought I would explode. For a brief moment, I swam in his memories. Memories of my mother, their love, their brief life together, his joy when they found out about me. His reading nursery rhymes to her belly, all the cherished memories that kept him alive all these years. Hope and horror comingled at his exile and every day under Samantha's thumb.

The light faded, but before it died with him, he bestowed on me one final gift. One he stole by ripping Samantha's throat open. He gave me every ounce of magic the witch harbored, along with what little was left of his.

"Starlight..." he whispered through a bubble of blood. Then his eyelids dropped closed, and he breathed his final breath.

The wall behind us began to spark. If it failed, the people would be at the mercy of these beasts. I wasn't sure they were aware of the danger because they still watched as if they couldn't tear their eyes away.

The Regent rolled onto her hands and knees, her breathing that of an animal, as blood dripped from her throat. My pack surrounded her, and the rest of the ravagers split their attention between the dying ruler and us. I was sure the fresh blood dripping from Jaden's arm captured their attention just as much as Samantha's soaking the ground.

One of the closer ravagers launched.

Before I could recite a spell to repel the beast, Jaden's strong command of "stop" filled the air. The beast stopped mid-air and then fell, dazed like he'd run into a brick wall.

The crowd behind the barrier gasped at his unusual display of power.

"We need to get out of here," he said, and his nose began trickling blood.

"We need to protect sector eleven."

He turned, and for the first time, saw the crumbling wall dividing the people from the beasts. When his gaze came back to mine, it was frantic.

"How?"

"I've seen the ancient spell books, Jaden. I know what to do, but I need your help. I need you to stop them from attacking while I fortify the barrier. Okay?" I said, praying he still had the strength to do what I asked.

"I think I can hold them off, but I'm not sure about her," he said, nodding at something behind my back.

I took a quick glance in time to see the pack attacking his mother. She was fighting back as the change took over in earnest. She was becoming another intelligent monster like my father had been, and something about that gave me a shiver. Even though I knew her magic had been stripped, the newly formed beast would be a foe to be wary of. All it took was one bite.

I met his gaze, took a deep breath, and went to reach for the barrier.

Jaden stepped in front of me, shaking his head. "You can't do that."

"Get out of my way. I need the power in the wall to do this."

"Even in this depleted state, it can still kill you," he said, glancing over my head at the restless pack.

"If I don't, they will turn our sector into a battle zone," I said, following his gaze as the pack closed in. "You have the ability to put up a barrier around us, so do it and let me protect the rest of the people."

"Star," he whispered, pleading.

"Shut the fuck up and make sure those things don't get to us."

He leaned over and caught a quick kiss. "If this doesn't work, if it kills you, I'm walking right into the middle of them. Understand?"

I paused and cupped his cheek. "I love you, too, but this isn't a suicide mission. Trust me. All I need is a few minutes, okay?"

He yielded and stepped to the side, dipping his head. With a deep breath, he inhaled, filling his chest enough so it puffed out. When his head rose, his eyes nearly glowed they were so green. "Stay."

The simple word created a ripple effect, and the beasts in our attack circle froze in place. I studied the handsome line of Jaden's jaw and the tremble of the muscles underneath as he used what little strength he had left to protect us.

With a deep breath of my own, I sent a silent plea to the gods asking for mercy. I swiped my hand across Jaden's torn shoulder, receiving a wince in response, and reached out. The electrical current tickled my blood-soaked fingers as I closed the distance. Then the full power of an electrical storm surrounded me. Instead of crippling me with pain or shutting down my heart, it fueled me, increasing the magic inside me a thousand fold.

I leaned my head back, screaming the incantation to the heavens.

"I call on thee, Hecate, Goddess of Witchcraft and Sorcery! Come to me, and be my shield. Banish these creatures, let this wall make them yield.

"I bind myself to thee with my love's blood. Give thy enemy the power to see the strength of the elements by my side. Rules of magic, I shall abide. I am bound to the beauty of the stars, the suns life-giving rays, the whiteness of the moon, the flash of lightning, the whirling wind, the stable earth, and the deep salt sea. Forge this barrier for me.

"Craft it in white fire. Weave it higher in shimmering flame. None shall come to hurt or maim. None with harmful intent shall pass this fiery wall. No evil shall pass... None at all!"

I reached out and grabbed Jaden's bound wrists, pulling him closer to me. The shimmer surrounded us. I closed my eyes, remembering the drawings of the sector, the maps, the boundaries, willing the wall to strengthen and expand to include its original borders.

Unfortunately, that included a good part of the field we stood in, leaving at least two dozen creatures on our side of the barrier, including his now feral mother. Before, it was only us at their mercy. Now it was the entire sector.

"Shit," I whispered.

Jaden's gaze moved to the newly formed wall beyond our unwanted visitors. "You need to get me out of these restraints."

I looked down and placed my hand on the cuffs. "What is now locked, let be unlocked."

Jaden pulled his hands free, rubbing his wrists before he turned to the shocked guards. Most of the weapons were pointed at him.

"Kill him," the Regent growled.

The guards' guns wavered, moving from his obvious human figure to her mutated ravager form. The confusion of seeing a ravager on two legs and talking reflected in the uniform creases between their eyes.

I needed to take control of the situation before the shock wore off and one side or the other cast the first stone.

"You are no longer in charge of this sector," I said to Samantha.

She hissed in response.

I scanned the beasts within the confines of our safety net, and every gaze except Samantha's met mine. "Freedom or death." I pointed towards the barrier. "Your choice."

The beasts that Samantha had caged as test subjects turned and ran right through the barrier, and never looked back. A few others joined them, but the majority of ravagers that had no clue what being confined to a cell for decades felt like seemed less keen on leaving their next meal on the table.

Samantha screamed and launched at us. Jaden put his hand out, and without words, he sent her tumbling backwards, ass over teakettle. The crowd gasped, but I was more worried about the remaining ravagers.

"Get those people back!" I yelled at the closest guard.

He just blinked at me and brought his gun up. I turned and tackled Jaden as a bullet whizzed by the spot where we had been standing.

A thud pulled my gaze behind me. A ravager lay sprawled less than three feet away with a bullet hole between his eyes. I scanned the field for Samantha. She was getting to her feet, licking her lips at the people near her.

Saliva ran from the corner of her mouth. The bloodlust had taken hold, and if someone didn't intervene, there would be more like her.

"White fire, claim the space between the innocent and the monster, now!" I pointed my finger, creating a line of lightning between the crowd and Samantha.

Both reared back in shock, and the sector eleven citizens realized this was not a game. The murmurs began, and then panic filled the air as people turned to flee from a fate more horrific than death.

The movement caught the ravagers' attention. Jaden pushed my head down as the line of guards opened fire.

When the shooting stopped, my ears rang as we looked up. The ravagers that had not fled back through the barrier lay dead on the field. And the only surviving beast on our side of the firewall was Samantha.

I scrambled to my feet, pulling Jaden up with me. The crowd's retreat slowed to a stop.

"You little bitch," she said, pointing at me. "I will ensure you suffer for your insubordination and subterfuge."

"What about the deception you've been executing for years?" I yelled. The anger welled up from the depths of my soul. "You killed my parents because you were jealous and just couldn't deal with rejection. In order to justify your scorn, you made up this ridiculous rule about male witches being evil." I turned to the crowd. "She exiled my father because he was not interested in her. She used her station as Regent to get rid of any opposition and exact her own personal revenge. It wasn't just. It was a bitter woman making sure no one would question her rule."

"Shut up, slave!" someone in the remaining crowd yelled. "You and that traitor must leave!"

The guards' weapons were now trained on us.

"Give them what they want," Jaden said.

I hesitated. If they didn't accept Jaden as the new Regent, then we couldn't make them. I gave him a nod and extinguished the flame between Samantha and the stragglers.

"If that's truly what you want, then I'll gladly give you your Regent." I waved at the beast thirty yards away then took Jaden's hand.

We took a few steps towards the barrier. Samantha stood watching, calculating. I could see the wheels in her head turning. I stopped, unable to sentence my sector to destruction.

"I can't," I whispered to Jaden.

"Exile them, and if they do not leave, kill them!" she ordered in that horrific growl.

Jaden's face reddened, and he glared at what once was his mother. "Why don't you come over here yourself and try to kill me?"

Samantha turned towards us, showing her teeth.

"One bite, Jaden. That's all it takes. She's not like the rest."

He glanced at me and then at the guards stubbornly keeping true to the last order they received.

"Screw them all," he whispered. Rage thrived in his eyes like a living being.

Panic flared again at the futility of the moment. I saved Jaden and the sector, and it was all going to shit because the guards couldn't think for themselves.

"He isn't evil. She is!" I pointed at the vile bitch approaching us like she was Lazarus risen from the dead. I turned to Jaden, knowing he lacked both the strength and dexterity in his current beaten condition to defeat Samantha. I grabbed him, pulling him into a kiss before planting my hands on either side of his head.

"By full moon's light, with helping hands, I spread good health throughout this man. Send energies far and near, to heal this form that I hold dear."

Jaden's eyes glowed green, and he winced as the healing spell took hold, fixing his ailments.

I let go and faced Samantha. "I am stronger than you can fathom. I lived through your twisted spells and poison potions when many others failed your tests." I positioned myself between Jaden and his mother. "And you know damn well I am of pure lineage."

A hush fell over the remaining crowd.

"You were my slave," she snarled.

"Because you knew my father came from the purest witch line in history, and when he refused you, you decided to exile him and enslave my mother, and me by default. My father didn't die at the hands of the ravagers. You sentenced him to a cell in the basement of your estate where you practiced your black magic spells on him, trying to extract the ability to temporarily control those beasts!" I pointed towards the barrier. "You turned him into something worse than a ravager. You turned him into a monster using their blood and your filthy spells."

Sparks formed on my fingertips, tingling as my caged fury ascended to a different level. "When you dragged him into that cell, the venom in his system was not strong enough to turn him. He was still human!" I bellowed, my voice carrying over the murmuring crowd.

"Give me a goddamned sword," Jaden said from behind me.

"You stole my life from me," I screamed. The power shot from my fingers, slamming right into the middle of Samantha's chest, and threw her back. The sudden surge left me dizzy and disoriented. I stumbled but Jaden caught me and gently set me on the ground.

His eyes glowed a shade of green that had always captivated me.

"I didn't know," he said softly.

"I know. I have every one of my father's memories. You were only trying to find a cure. The real monster has always been your mother."

A guard approached. "I'm sorry, but the court..." He glanced at Jaden. "The court ruling still stands."

I forced myself into a sitting position at the same time Samantha did across the field. "If you exile Jaden, I will go with him, and if he dies, I die. And when I die, your precious barrier disintegrates."

The guard's face paled, and he glanced at the thing still holding the current Regency.

"She has no magic to fix this. My father saw to that."

His gaze flew to mine, and his eyes widened.

"Are you willing to sentence all of sector eleven to death, or worse, to becoming mutated ravagers like her?" Jaden asked.

The guard sucked his lower lip in between his teeth as he glanced at Samantha. He shifted and shook his head.

Samantha had started towards us again, but one of the crowd came within arm's reach. Her teeth sunk into the idiot's face, drawing blood before she dropped him to the ground. He screamed as the plague burned away his humanity.

Samantha smiled and wiped her mouth.

"Give me the sword," Jaden said, putting his hand out. The deadly quality in his tone matched that in his eyes.

The guard glanced at the screaming man while unclasping the steel from his belt and then handed it to Jaden.

"Whoever she bites has to be killed. Beheaded works better than bullets. Understand?" he said to the guard.

The guard nodded and spoke into his comms, issuing the order to kill that poor soul writhing on the ground.

Jaden met my gaze. "Even if it's me."

I shook my head, but he was up on his feet, wielding the sword like a true warrior before I could stop him.

Samantha's lunatic smile chilled me as much as the long razor sharp claws that once were her fingers. She uttered the words to one of the ancient spells asking for the power and agility of the gods. Dark clouds formed overhead as the blackest of magic swirled.

My father may have stripped her magical essence, but she still knew how to call on the dark elements. And it looked like they were responding.

The years of hiding in that locked room reading the ancient collections came in handy. I knew how to counteract those dark elements.

I laid my hands on the earth, closing my eyes, summoning the mother to rise up and banish the blackness forming over our heads. "May mother earth destroy the darkness, with all her might and grace!"

The ground rumbled, rippling under my hands and outward. A fissure started between my fingertips, spreading over the field like angry tentacles. White light bled from the earth, shooting at the storm clouds overhead.

Samantha charged. So did Jaden. Her roar made my stomach clench in terror. Instead of running her though with the blade, Jaden dropped into a slide, ducking under the deadly arch of her claws. He rolled and was up on his feet facing her as she spun around.

His expression was unreadable, but his eyes glowed green, even at this distance. He swung the sword. Samantha bent away from the blow, hissing as the blade drew a thin line of blood across her chest.

My internal alarms started, and a jolt of adrenaline shot though my form, turning my icy veins into burning fuel. I had no idea why the sirens in my head were screaming, but I found myself running toward Jaden. Out of instinct, I reached for the nearest guard's sword and yanked it from its sheath.

Jaden's face had gone red in frustration. He swung again. Samantha sidestepped and knocked Jaden off balance. He hit the ground and lost his grip on the sword. Samantha lunged. Jaden kicked. His foot planted right into Samantha's stomach, knocking her on her ass. He rolled and started scrambling away.

My heart leapt into my throat, pounding a frantic drumbeat from the rush of blood operating on high octane.

Samantha caught his foot and sunk her teeth into his ankle.

One bite... The thought nearly dropped me.

Jaden's growling howl echoed. His other foot connected with his mother's face and she flew backwards.

I swung my sword. The blade whistled though the air and cut clean through Jaden's leg, just below the knee. The impact with the ground vibrated all the way from the tip of the blade to my arms. I stood and spun, swinging the sword with me. The speed and strength filling every cell wasn't enough.

The force of Samantha's body hitting me knocked me on the ground. I managed to roll her off and climb to my feet before I realized her head was still rolling three feet away, cut clean off by my blade.

My breath filled my ears as the sirens inside me subsided. Jaden grimaced, holding the hemorrhaging stump of his leg. The sword fell from my hand. I yanked the sash from the coat I wore and dropped to my knees to try to tie a tourniquet around his thigh.

A high buzz filled my head as my heartbeat returned to normal, and with it came the after shakes of a fading adrenaline rush. I yanked on the ends of the belt, tightening the tourniquet until the flow of blood slowed.

His pained gaze found mine. "What have you done?"

"I saved your life," I said, but his eyes still blazed with fury. He couldn't possibly be mad at me, could he?

"You cut off my fucking leg!" he yelled, confirming my thought.

"You're damn right. It's better than having to cut off your head." I pointed at his blackened bare foot lying a few feet away. Mutated ravager skin matched that of Samantha's dead body a few feet away.

Instead of dealing with his aggravation, I concentrated on creating a small ball of fire in my hand. When the flame burned blue, I slammed it into the end of his stump, cauterizing the blood vessels and stopping any further loss of blood.

He bellowed in pain, clutching his hands into fists. His panting finally slowed, and he opened his eyes at what was left of his leg. "You should have killed me." His voice held a measure of contempt aimed at me.

I sat back on the ground, my strength draining as the sky cleared. Numbness overtook me as I stared at him. I opened my mouth several times, but I couldn't muster an apology. I was not sorry, and I wouldn't say something I didn't mean.

"You cut my leg off," he said again, waving at the obvious.

Heat boiled through my numbness like a volcano erupting. "It's not like I cut your dick off," I snapped.

His eyebrows rose. He did the same thing I had, the opening and closing of the mouth, before he pressed his lips together.

I'd rendered him speechless.

"You made me into a cripple," he finally said.

I rolled my eyes and stood up. "Would you rather I let you turn?" My hands found my hips as I stared down at him.

He glanced at his dead mother and sighed.

I turned to the guards just staring at the two of us. "Help me get the Regent to the hospital, please."

When their gazes landed on Samantha, I cleared my throat and pointed at Jaden.

"Excuse me?" Jaden said.

"As Samantha Mallory's only living relative, you assume the position," I said and turned back to the guards. "It's written in the law books." When no one moved, I added, "I can show you the original sector laws if you don't believe me."

The elite guards stepped forward, lifting Jaden from the ground.

"Lock her up until I can figure out what to do with her," Jaden said, sending a glare in my direction.

The remaining guards surrounded me, taking me by the arms. When they led me back down to the holding cells, I was relieved when they put me in the room across from the elevator. It had a cot, a sink, a toilet, and enough distance from where I was meant to die to find some comfort.

I collapsed onto the cot, letting the mind-numbing exhaustion take control.

Chapter 23

"Star?"

A soft plea pulled me out of a sound sleep.

I turned, surprised to see Jaden standing on a pair of crutches outside the bars. It had been weeks since he locked me up. The guards had brought me regular meals, water, clean clothes every day, and allowed me to take a shower every couple of days, so my prison term hadn't been all that hard.

Just lonely.

He glanced at the ground, and his jaw tensed. "They say you spared me," he finally said, but his voice was gruff and distant. When he raised his gaze, I saw the bitterness in the set of his lips. "Why?"

"Because I can't fathom a life where you aren't in it." I stood and approached the bars. "Why did you take so long to come see me?" But from the set of his jaw, I knew.

"I'm angry, Star. I'm fucking pissed, and I don't know how to get past this fury."

"Why?" I needed to hear the reason, because to me, losing part of a limb was easier to swallow than losing my life or the life of someone I loved.

He shook his head and looked up at the ceiling, struggling to articulate. "Because you didn't give me the choice."

My skin tingled with shock. I searched his sharp gaze. "Time wasn't exactly in your favor." Didn't he understand there was no other choice?

He leveled a glare.

"If it had been me, what would you have done?" I wrapped my hands around the bars, waiting for him to answer.

Jaden pressed his lips together and shrugged. "I've tried to put myself in your shoes, and I just can't. I can't envision doing anything that would leave you crippled for the rest of your life."

I stared at him and let out a laugh. "So, if it had been me, you would have killed me? Or worse, kept me locked up in a cell for the rest of my life?"

"I can find a cure," he said, but there was no conviction in his voice. "Besides I could never harm you. Not like this." He waved at his leg.

"Yet you bashed the hell out of my ribs and nearly raped me just so I'd have no fight left when your mother let the ravagers loose in my cell." The words tumbled out before I could stop them.

Hurt flared in his eyes, but I refused to look away. "I wasn't in control," he hissed, stepping closer. "You were."

"What I did was to save you, not destroy you."

He looked down at the ground, and his knuckles whitened on the handles of the crutches. The clench of his hands formed tight knots in his forearms, making the veins stand out. "I don't know what to believe anymore."

I stepped back from the cell bars. The lost look in his eyes amidst the frustration wasn't going to get resolved today. He needed to work out his issues, and based on my snap, I obviously had some issues of my own to deal with.

"How long are you going to keep me in this cell?"

His eyebrow arched. "We both know you could have left anytime."

He was right. I could have left, but if I had, I would have infuriated him further, and we might never get through whatever barriers we both had built since that night.

I shrugged. "You ordered me to be locked up."

His lips twitched and he nodded.

"Besides, where the hell would I go?"

He opened his mouth as if to answer and then closed it. "Point taken. Was this a revenge thing?" He pointed to his leg.

"Jaden, if I hadn't done that..." I couldn't continue. My throat tightened and my eyes misted. "They would have had to kill you." I blinked the tears away, refusing to let him see me cry. Not with the chill radiating from him.

"Would you really have been sad?"

His callous tone and darkening eyes shot through the misery gripping me, turning on the fire within.

"You have the audacity to ask me that? What the fuck is wrong with you?"

"Open," he growled and the door swung open with a bang. He crutched into the entry. "Take a good long look at what's wrong with me!" he yelled. His entire form shook.

I realized just how damaged his mother had left him. I stepped forward.

"Don't," he warned.

I ignored him and closed the distance until I stood close enough that only a sheet of paper could fit between us. He trembled and his eyes filled with tears before he blinked them away.

"I don't care that part of your leg is gone. It doesn't make me love you any less," I said, homing in on the insecurities plaguing him.

"What makes you think I care if you love me or not?" The hardness in his features caught me by surprise. "What makes you think I give a shit about a little slutty slave girl?"

I started to step back, but Jaden reached out and grabbed a handful of my hair. He pulled me to his lips, and the kiss was angry and rough, just like the grip he had on my hair. The crutch slammed on the floor, making both of us jump apart.

His chest rose and fell in unison with mine.

"I don't know whether to beat you or fuck you," he said with enough venom to make my stomach roll.

I pushed away from him. "Don't be such a dick."

For the first time since he walked in, he actually cracked a smile, and I saw a glimpse of the old Jaden. "I guess I should count my blessings that I still have one," he said and leaned down to pick up the crutch. "You are free to go."

"Where?"

"Anywhere but here," he said.

I blinked at the numbing shock, wondering if everything to this point had been a farce. My gaze dropped, falling on the ring on my hand and so many empty promises.

"So this?" I lifted my hand, showing him the ring I still wore.

He put his hand out. "I'll take that back."

There was no hint of a joke in his voice or gaze.

My chest squeezed in response, and I nearly doubled over with the pain his words caused. I worked the ring off my finger and threw it at him before I crossed to the elevator. It wasn't the exit I was hoping for, especially when he crutched next to me in front of the doors.

"I'd rather not have to share the elevator with you right now," I said, trying to keep the shake out of my tone. I couldn't peg the volatility of emotions swirling through me. A symphony of sensations from numbness to sharp pain struck every cell to the point I wasn't sure if I would shatter into a million tiny shards. I certainly did not want Jaden to witness my breakdown.

"Tough shit. I would rather have my leg back. Looks like neither of us is going to get what we want today."

The elevator ride was brutal. I was barely able to hold it together, and all he did was stare at the floor counter. When the elevator arrived at the main floor, I nearly sprinted from the lift. I did not want to walk with him, not with the unshed tears blinding me.

The stairs outside were slick enough that I almost slid down them instead of running. My brain knew where I was heading, and my heart ached by the time I stepped into the frigid lobby of our broken down building.

I climbed the stairs two at a time and stopped on the level where the room protected by my charms was located. My mother's blanket still lay on the bedding untouched. I grabbed it, slinging it over my shoulder as I tried to block the assault of memories from the room. Jaden making love to me was still embedded in the air. I backed out of the room, trading warmth for the chill outside. I climbed to our rooftop sanctuary with the blanket slung over my shoulder and settled with my back to an old vent box.

With the blanket wrapped around me, I watched the stars travel across the sky through a veil of tears. My mind kept shuffling through everything that happened leading up to this moment, and with each fond memory of Jaden, my heart hurt a little more. The cold stare he had given me was nothing I had ever seen on him. It was as if his soul died when I cut off the poisoned part of his leg.

When the sun broke the horizon, I wiped my face and lay down, closing my eyes against the growing brightness.

I dozed restlessly until my bladder and stomach demanded attention. It didn't take long to stow the blanket away before I climbed down the staircase and ventured out into the town proper for the first time since I was deemed an outcast.

The reception I received was a complete turnaround from being shunned. Just a few days ago, I was treated like a leper or worse, and now being treated like a royal princess was a little hard to swallow. People fell over themselves offering kindness and whatever I might need. I had never seen this kind of reception, not even when the Regent went out in public.

When I was offered a room at the most elegant hotel in our part of the sector, I almost turned it down. But I wasn't a fool. If I couldn't deal with my little shelter last night, I knew it would be just as difficult facing those memories tonight. Besides, I was curious to see how the other half lived.

The hotel manager led me into the penthouse suite, and I stared at the pure luxury surrounding me. The living space was bigger than both my mother's and Gypsy's entire apartments combined. The view out the window gave me the same view as my rooftop oasis, but this space had no frigid wind whipping through it. I slowly crossed to the adjoining bedroom and gawked at the massive four-poster bed.

It was far more elegant than even the Regent's quarters in the mansion, and it smelled like roses, strawberries, and clean linens.

"I can't possibly stay here," I said as I looked around the room and back to the manager.

"Is there something wrong with the accommodations?" The manager's brow furrowed.

I smiled to ease his worry. "No, sir. This is just...too much." I waved at the elaborate room, my cheeks heating. "Don't get me wrong, this is gorgeous. I've never seen a more beautiful place, but I'm used to servant quarters. Besides, I don't have the money to pay for this."

"Miss Brighton, this is on us."

I gaped at him, unable to speak as a nagging feeling surfaced. A few days ago these people were ready to feed me to the ravagers. "Why?"

His soft smile unarmed me. "Because you rebuilt the barrier before it failed. But more importantly, you've given us all hope that perhaps our persecution may be nearing an end."

I blinked at him. "What persecution?"

"You freed us from Samantha Mallory's black reign."

I had no idea the citizens felt the same way I did about their prior ruler. I guess being a servant in the mansion and having such limited access to the world outside had isolated me from the people.

"For decades, both the men and women of this sector have walked on egg shells. Making the Regent unhappy meant certain death, and the woman Master Mallory was betrothed to seemed to be worse than the Regent. As much as I don't condone what Master Mallory did, I have to say the collective sector breathed a sigh of relief when she disintegrated." He paused and glanced out the window. "Now with both Samantha Mallory and her heir apparent gone, the blackness over sector eleven seems to have been lifted. We just pray her son is more reasonable than she was."

I kept my lips closed against the need to defend Jaden in any way. Not with the way he treated me last night. He would have to build his own legacy, without my input. My heart squeezed. I joined the hotel manager's prayers that he wouldn't turn into a royal bastard.

"So, please, the city, as well as the sector, owe you their lives. Let me at least repay the kindness as best I can."

How could I refuse without offending this man? "Thank you."

He bowed and then left. I crossed to the bathroom and gazed at the tub. It was huge. I turned on the hot water, opened one of the bath salts, and dropped a couple in the water. Lavender and vanilla wafted from the soapy water. I stripped, tossing my dirty clothes onto the bed before taking advantage of the tub.

Slipping into that bath was like stepping into heaven. Buttons on the lip of the tub intrigued me, so I pushed one. The water became a ripple of bubbles, and jets pounded into my back. I tensed but after a moment, the pulse hit several different spots, creating a pleasant tingling like a good massage.

I leaned back and closed my eyes, enjoying a luxury I had never had a chance to experience before. By the time I finally stepped out of the remaining suds, my fingers and toes had turned to wrinkled prunes. A bathrobe hung on the back of the door, and I slipped it on, relishing the soft terry against my skin.

I stepped into the room, not really interested in getting back into the clothing I slept in, and stopped. Two women stood waiting for me, one blonde and the other a tall redhead. Both were wearing hotel attire of black and white, and one had a binder in her hand.

"Miss Brighton, we are here to escort you to the spa," the tall redhead with the binder said. She snapped the notebook closed and offered me a beaming smile.

I wrapped the bathrobe a little tighter, unaccustomed to having anyone serve me, much less offer me a spa day. "I'm sorry, but I think the bubble bath and room are enough."

They traded a glance, and I caught something akin to an 'I told you so' between them.

The redhead sighed. "I'm afraid the manager insists."

"Why in the world is everyone treating me like royalty?" I asked.

"Because you stood up to the Regent. You stopped the exile of good men just because they did not bend to the whim of a bitter woman," the short blonde said.

In some ways, her severe profile reminded me of Eleanor, but the kindness in her eyes told me she was not made of the same rough cloth as that evil witch.

"I'm not sure Jaden Mallory warranted saving, but you stopped his mother, so we are all relieved and grateful. And we understand it is you who is protecting the sector now," she added, her voice taking on a softer quality to match the warmth in her eyes.

My eyebrows rose, and I thought my mouth may have popped open at the comment about Jaden, but I focused on the last statement and gave a shrug like it wasn't a big deal. It had been easy in retrospect.

"So, now we have been tasked with your care." The redhead smiled.

I shifted and pulled the robe tighter. "What are your names?"

"Nancy," said the tall redhead.

"Anne," said the shorter blonde.

"Well, Nancy and Anne, I have to be honest. The thought of being pampered is something completely foreign to me and a bit uncomfortable."

"Girl, I know what you are feeling," Anne said. "I've been there, but I promise you will forget about being uncomfortable the moment you sit in the pedicure chair. By the time we bring you back to your room, you will feel like a brand new woman."

Just by the insistent, but kind, looks on their faces, I knew I wasn't going to get out of this. I stepped towards where I had left my clothes and paused. My jeans and sweater were gone. Instead, a pair of lacy white undergarments lay in their place.

"Your clothing has been taken to the laundry, and they will be returned long before you are."

Nancy winked at me. "The undergarments are from our finest line, and they are here for your comfort, but truly the bathrobe is all you need for the spa. We will wait if you are more comfortable with undergarments on."

The thought of being naked and vulnerable in any way after what I went through in Samantha's jail wasn't welcomed. There would be no relaxation if I didn't have some kind of barrier between me and the unknown.

I gave them a nod and took the underwear and bra into the bathroom. The satin and lace felt divine. I pulled the bathrobe back over my shoulders before relinquishing myself to their plans.

Chapter 24

They hadn't been kidding. I sat in a massage chair while my feet soaked in a hot fragrant tub and girls worked on massaging my arms and legs. Each calf was rubbed with a gritty substance and then washed clean before the pedicurist wrapped my legs in a hot towel.

Whatever discomfort I had at being pampered evaporated, and I closed my eyes, enjoying the sensations of the filing boards on my nails. It seemed like forever before they transferred me to the hairdressing section. I kept staring at my perfectly manicured nails while the hairdresser chatted aimlessly about the weather, about the to-do from the other night, and the regency scandal.

I shifted, acutely aware that I was at the center of that scandal, and these women really had no idea.

"Can you believe he concocted a spell to kill his own bride?" the hairdresser said.

"He didn't," I said very quietly.

"Excuse me, hon, did you say something?" she asked, leaning over so she could see my face.

"Jaden didn't cast that spell. It was cast as a means to protect him from someone with nefarious intent."

They laughed uncomfortably and traded glances. "How do you know this?"

I sighed. "Because I cast it."

The hairdresser stopped curling my hair and met my gaze. "Why on earth would you do that?"

"To protect him from marrying someone as cold-hearted as his mother. Someone who would exile him at the first chance."

"But why? Why would you protect such an ass?"

I couldn't help the laugh that tumbled from my lips. "Why do you think he's an ass?"

"That man has no heart," she said, and her lips thinned as she went back to curling my hair.

I stared at her, waiting for more of an explanation. After a few minutes of silence, I raised an eyebrow, silently prompting her for more.

"I knew him in college," she said. "He had a way of disarming every woman around him, and most fell over themselves to get into his bed. While he took all of us up on our offers, he always kept emotional distance, like his soul belonged elsewhere." She took another section of my hair and wrapped it around the curling iron. "A lot of girls fell in love with him. Me included."

I could identify with exactly how she felt.

"But after he got what he wanted, which was just a good lay, he shut each of us out and moved on to the next girl who would spread her legs." She gave a small shrug. "I guess maybe after finding out he had magic in his blood, it makes sense, but he still didn't need to be an asshole about everything."

This conversation was giving me more insight into Jaden than I cared to have. It looked like what he was doing with me was the same thing he did with all the other girls that came before. Get me to bed then cut me loose.

I kept my feelings out of the conversation, but they churned in my stomach, stuck somewhere between hurt and angry. I would have laid my life down for Jaden. Hell, I walked through the barrier to save him, and he treated me like this?

Maybe they were right. Maybe he was just an asshole.

Something deep down inside me scoffed at the thought.

I shifted in the chair. "He used to be my closest friend, and he's not too happy with me for cutting off his leg."

"So that's true?" She gasped while continuing to style my hair.

"Yes. It was either that or let the ravager venom turn him. I made a choice, and it pissed him off."

Another woman stepped in front of me, interrupting the conversation, and I welcomed the distraction. When she opened her bag, I got a peek inside.

"Makeup?"

She smiled and nodded. "It's part of the package."

"Okay, but please just keep it natural looking. I don't want to look like a painted whore."

"Absolutely," she said and rolled a seat next to me.

Powders, blushes, and eye shadow brushes caressed my face, relaxing me further. When she finished, she gave a nod to the hairdresser and they twirled me around. The view in the mirror made me smile. It reminded me of the way Gypsy made me look, except it wasn't a glamour. This was *me* in the mirror.

"Wow." I couldn't think of anything to say beyond that.

"Do you like?" the hairdresser asked.

I nodded. "It's just...I have never..." I waved towards the mirror and smiled up at them. "Thank you."

It was too bad that only the people in this room would see their hard work. I climbed out of the chair and headed out of the wonderful spa with Nancy and Anne.

They led me inside my room, parting as they entered and let me step between them. In the center of the room sat a luggage dolly with a white dress hanging from the bar.

An elegant white wedding dress.

A chill ran down my spine. I turned and the figure sitting on the edge of the bed wearing a black suit caught my breath. It was Jaden.

"Give me five minutes," he said, and the girls high-tailed it out of the room.

His green eyes pierced through me, and everything fell into place.

"I still don't know what to believe. I haven't been able to decide if you are what I always believed you were, or if you are worse than my mother ever was."

"Jaden." I took a step in his direction, but his hand went up, stopping me.

"I heard everything you accused my mother of. If you knew those things all this time—"

"When my father transferred his magic, he transferred his memories," I said. "I had no idea that he was still alive when your mother had him locked up. If I had known that… You're right, I could have never abided what she did, and either your mother or I would have died years ago."

He stood and grabbed the crutches. That was when I noticed the black suit he wore wasn't a suit at all. It was a finely fitted tuxedo. My gaze shot to the wedding dress, and my heart jumped in my chest.

"I hope for your sake that you are telling me the truth." He glanced at the watch on his wrist. "Because in exactly thirty minutes, your intentions will be put to the test."

I blinked at him. "Excuse me?" My hands found my hips.

"This is the only way I can be sure about you. If your intentions aren't pure, you'll end up like Eleanor."

"Fuck you. I'm not marrying you today." Aggravation welled up inside me alongside the conflicting exhilaration at actually marrying Jaden. But this was nothing like the dream. It was nothing like our 'what if' conversation in the jail cells. This wasn't the way it was supposed to be between us.

"Yes. You are. And if you run, I swear I will hunt you down and cut out your lying tongue before I lock you up for the rest of your life." His glare chilled me to the core.

"You want to marry someone you don't love? That makes no sense."

"Nothing makes sense to me right now, so this is just par for the course."

"Do you love me?"

He stared at me and then slowly shook his head. "I don't know. I thought I did, and if you are the same girl I forced to tell me the truth on top of our building, then I will happily pledge my future to you. But if you aren't..." He shrugged.

I crossed my arms. "This isn't exactly how I envisioned being proposed to."

He crutched over to me. "I don't really give a damn. This is how it's going to be."

"You did all this?" I twirled my finger around the room and then at my face and hair.

His lips pressed tighter, but the tell-tale dimple appeared for a brief moment along with a reddening hue. "The girl I thought I loved would have kicked my ass if I sprung this on her without letting her have some prep," he said and headed to the door.

"Jaden?"

He stopped but didn't turn. "I'm giving you the chance to prove to me that everything you've ever said is true." Then he left.

The dress was perfection on a hanger and everything I did not want. I didn't want to be forced into marriage, even if it was Jaden standing at the end of the aisle.

Nancy and Anne stepped in a moment later, their eyes averted.

"So, all this?" I waved at my face. I didn't need to say more. Not when their entire faces turned crimson.

"Yes, ma'am," they both said in unison and restlessly shifted in place.

"We were told that if we blew it, it would mean our jobs," Anne burst out.

"Jaden told you that?" I wouldn't put it past him, not with the ultimatum he just issued.

"No, ma'am, our boss did," Nancy said, sending a glare in Anne's direction.

"I think I'll need to have to have a talk with your boss after the wedding."

Both their gazes landed on mine.

"I'm assuming that's why you're here. To make sure I make it to the ceremony." They nodded and I rolled my eyes. "I'm not going to run."

"Aren't you worried about the curse?" Nancy asked.

"What curse?"

"The one that killed his last wife?"

I chuckled. Neither of them had been in the salon when I had the conversation with the hairdresser. "No. I'm not worried in the least. That was a protection spell, not a curse. And he didn't cast it."

They traded a confused glance and then looked back at me.

"I saved his ass because I wasn't about to see an innocent man persecuted for my mistake."

"Your mistake?"

"Why in god's name do you think I was stupid enough to run outside the barrier?"

They exchanged another glance and shrugged.

"I cast the spell. I was trying to protect the man, but it backfired." I turned to the dress. "And now I have to marry him, not because we both want this, but because he is insisting on proof I wasn't out for revenge when I maimed him and killed his mother." I sighed. "So, let's get this thing on."

They hustled to my side and helped me into the tailored satin. The dress fit like it had been specially made for me. I stepped in front of a full length mirror to inspect the final presentation. The image was as stunning as the glamour had been when I attended his last wedding.

I stared into my dark eyes, wondering why I was going through with this. Why was I letting him corner me this way? And on the heels of that thought, I wondered if I would pass my own test.

I wasn't sure if all the hurt and anger brewing in my heart would taint my intentions. My heart was still his, even though I didn't want to admit it. But was that enough? Were my reasons pure enough not to be turned to cinder?

If I ran, he would find me. I only had one hiding place, and he knew it well enough to navigate it on crutches. Besides, if I made that choice, he would never forgive me. The anger in his eyes when he issued his threat would be realized, and I believed he would follow through with every word of it.

But that wasn't what my heart wanted, even though my mind was resisting this.

I couldn't run away.

I couldn't say no.

I couldn't lose Jaden, even with the ultimatum he had set forth.

I'd just have to see if what was in my heart was enough.

Chapter 25

I stood outside the looming doors of the grand ballroom on edge. Nerves bit at my skin, and I chewed my lip. I held a beautiful rose bouquet and shifted from foot to foot.

"Are you okay?" Anne asked as she straightened my train.

I gave her a nod, but I wasn't okay. I was terrified, and it had nothing to do with the curse. It was the realization of a dream that I had had for years.

I was actually marrying Jaden Mallory. Under duress, but I was actually going to be his wife.

A light sweat broke out on my exposed back. I stifled a shiver.

The doors opened, and I stared into the dark room filled with strangers. A spotlight shined on the altar. Jaden stepped into view with a single crutch. When his eyes met mine, everything around me disappeared.

Hope. Fear. Anger. Lust. A rainbow of emotions resided in that single glance.

I swallowed the lump in my throat, and my feet moved forward on shaking legs.

I stopped next to him, and his gaze moved from head to toe and back. The smile I was accustomed to flashed, along with a spark in his eyes. He pressed his lips together, squashing the glimpse of happiness before he took my hand and maneuvered onto the altar.

My heart raced as the minister started the ceremony. Jaden kept my hand tight in his, like he thought I might flee at any moment. Everything moved in a blur, even our vows. Jaden didn't hesitate when asked if he took me as his wife. His 'I do' was firm and loud enough to fill the ballroom.

When it was my turn to pledge my life to this man, I caught his gaze and took a deep breath. The eyes looking back at me were full of the old Jaden I knew, and not the prick I had been exposed to in the last couple of days. When I didn't answer right away, his hands squeezed mine, hard, as fear raced across his eyes.

"I do," I said loud enough for only the minister and Jaden to hear.

Jaden's grip on my hands loosened, and the tightness in his jaw relaxed. He blew a slow stream of air out like he had been holding it in until that very moment. A soft smile found his lips.

When the minister asked for the rings, Jaden pulled two out of his pocket. I had less than a second to register what was in the minister's hand before I glanced at Jaden. He held the diamond Jaden took from me yesterday. A dimple appeared in Jaden's cheek, but he didn't look at me. He was too focused on the minister.

As soon as the minister blessed the rings, he turned to Jaden, offering him my wedding band.

"Repeat after me," the minister ordered.

"With this ring, I thee wed," Jaden said, repeating the minister's instructions, and slid the band onto my finger.

The diamond solitaire was soldered together with a diamond studded band. I sighed as I stared at it. The lengths Jaden went through for this moment conflicted with his ultimatum. Everything he did took time to prepare.

The minister interrupted my musings with a clearing of his throat, and I took the ring he offered. Jaden's band was heavy with a single diamond chip embedded in the black gold.

"Repeat after me," the minister said.

"With this ring, I thee wed," I said and pushed Jaden's band onto his left ring finger. Then I looked up into his sparkling green eyes.

For a moment, I thought this might be a dream, but the moment the minister announced us husband and wife and instructed Jaden to kiss his bride, that thought shattered.

Dread filled Jaden's eyes. His hands squeezed mine. I stepped closer so he wouldn't need to.

He dropped my left hand and cupped my cheek. His gaze dropped from my eyes to my lips. I licked them, smoothing out the sudden dryness. He leaned close and paused.

"I love you, Star," he whispered. The dread in his eyes filled his voice. He closed the distance.

His warm lips covered mine in such tender tentativeness that my heart melted. It was sweet and scared all in one motion. He pulled back, still cupping my cheek.

I opened my eyes and met his gaze. The entire room sat silent waiting for me to become a pile of ashes. I waited as well, giving my fate to the gods. If they deemed me unworthy, I would follow in Eleanor's path.

I think I counted to ten before the spark in Jaden's eyes ignited and his lips were on mine again. This time it was hungry and intense. I opened my mouth welcoming his tongue dance that set my body on fire.

The room erupted in applause, startling both of us. The kiss broke and so did the magic of the moment. His soft gaze hardened as he looked out at the crowd. The music started, and he grabbed my hand, crutching out of the ballroom with no acknowledgement of the clapping.

I glanced at him as we headed for the elevator. "No reception?"

"No. I didn't feel like celebrating with a bunch of strangers that were so hell bent on seeing me die less than a month ago."

I understood his aversion, but the people of the sector were truly poisoned by Samantha's rule and only doing what they believed she wanted. She had proven so many times that if someone stepped off that path, she would destroy them. It wasn't a personal choice; it was self-preservation. Of that I was sure, especially after the conversations I had today both in the street and within this hotel.

I followed him up to the penthouse in silence. He swiped his card key and held the door for me, following after I stepped inside. In the center of the room sat a small table that held a wedding cake along with a bottle of champagne. I smiled. He had thought of almost everything, and it warmed my heart.

The door closed, and he leaned against it with his back to me. The tension in his shoulders and back stood out in the tight fabric of his tuxedo. Whatever demons he had held at bay downstairs during our vows came back.

"Can I at least have a first dance with you?" I asked. There were still some wedding traditions I believed in, and the first dance was one I was not willing to forgo because of his anger or his ego.

He glared over his shoulder. "Is that a joke?"

"No. It isn't. You're more than capable of balancing on one foot." I waited in the center of the room.

His eyebrow rose, but he crutched over to me. "I'm still pissed." Even his voice was filled with the bitter anger he still held onto.

"Dance with me first, then we can talk."

"Star..." he started, but I didn't care.

I ensnared his neck with my arms and pressed my body against his. Reluctantly, he wrapped his free arm around my waist, pulling me closer.

"There's no music."

"I don't care." I put my head on his shoulder and just swayed slowly in place.

The warmth of the moment penetrated every cell, and being this close to him turned my nerve centers into a collection of sensations. Summer rain filled my nostrils as I inhaled his fresh scent. The softness of his cheek against my forehead lulled my eyes closed. His hand ran gently over my exposed back.

"Is this real?" I whispered.

He huffed a laugh, and his body went rigid again. "Doesn't fell like it, does it?"

"No." I looked up at him. "Why did you do all this?"

"Because no matter how angry I am, I realized I need you." He glanced away and broke contact, almost pushing me from his arms. "Which pisses me off even more." He crutched to the chair near the window and collapsed in it.

I took the seat next to him. "So your little declaration downstairs that you love me was all for show?"

He stared out at the dark remnants of the city and sighed. "No. But I honestly thought you were going to turn to dust. I thought you snowed me just like you had snowed my mother for all those years. But then again, it's your spell, so who the hell knows."

"Jaden, I'm still that girl you followed up to the top of that high rise. I'm still the girl you made love to in that little storage room."

He glanced over at me. "But I'm not that guy anymore."

"Why, because you lost part of your leg?"

"No, because everything I believed was destroyed in one moment. I thought my mother loved me, but that was a farce. I thought the council would believe me when I told them I didn't kill Eleanor, but that was a fantasy. And I thought Frankenstein was just a mutated ravager, even though the science never added up. Now it all makes perfect sense, but the fact that I doubted the scientific facts means my belief in my abilities to discern fact from fiction is crap. And above all, my mother was truly the monster in this little fairytale, so what the hell does that make me?"

I listened to his rant and kept my gaze on the cityscape, watching his reflection in the glass. I let the question hang in the air because I saw a little of the monster he was capable of becoming when he was under Samantha's control.

"Star?" he said after the silence became uncomfortable.

I turned, meeting his gaze. "I don't know. It depends on what path you choose, Jaden. I can't change what happened to either of us. I can only move forward and fight whatever demons seem to exist between us. But I can't do that alone. It takes two people to make a relationship work, and neither of us knows what that looks like. All I know is I won't be your slave, and I don't expect you to be mine."

It was his turn to be silent as he mulled over my words. "And if I somehow am destined to become a monster?"

I rolled my eyes at him. "That's a choice, not a destiny. If you choose to be a monster, then I will not stand by you, despite the pledge I just made in front of all those people."

He balked. "Are you serious?"

"Yes. I'm dead serious. If you choose to be a cold-hearted bastard, then we have a problem."

His hands clenched the chair arms, and his jaw line jumped with tension. "There are times I just want to smack you."

His glare lit my own aggravation. I stood. "Then let's go. Let's see what you can do." I waved him in like a sparring partner in the ring.

He continued to glare at me from the chair. "You'd hit a cripple?"

"You bet your ass. Just like you have it in you to beat the shit out of a woman." I knew it was a low blow, but it came out with such ferocity that Jaden's eyes narrowed.

He stood and stepped in, crowding me, his green eyes holding a wave of darkness like I'd never seen. "You really want to do this?"

My fists clenched. "I want payback." My eyes widened at the subconscious slip. I knew I had some issues to deal with, but the conversation was bringing forth some ugly feelings.

His eyebrows rose. "For what?"

"For the shit you put me through." My hand jumped to my mouth. I glared at him as the burn of anger ran through my blood. "You did it again, didn't you?"

He actually smiled and pulled the mint sprig out of his cheek, tossing it on the edge of the table. "Damn straight."

The bastard plied me with truth serum. "What about you? You really want to do this?"

"No. I want to rip that dress off and have angry sex with you until neither of us can think," he growled. His eyes sparkled.

If I was under a spell, he certainly had to be too. My eyes narrowed as I studied him. "You're affected by this as well, aren't you?"

"Yes. It's the only way I could think of beyond the wedding to figure out how much of this is real. Why do you think I'm babbling like a fucking idiot?"

Anger rose from the depths of my heart and I swung. He was ready and grabbed my wrist, pulling me against him.

"I'm pissed at you for everything you did to me," I yelled, struggling in his grip. "You had this entire town shun me, and then when we were in that cell, you beat the shit out of me. If I hadn't head-butted you, you would have raped me." It all came forth like a giant surge. "I'm also mad because you just gave up. You were going to let those filthy beasts tear you apart without a fight." Tears sprung to my eyes. "And I'm angry that I had to hurt you. I never wanted to do that, but I couldn't let you turn and be killed. Hell, I didn't even know if it would work." I tried to push away from him, but he held fast, bracing himself with the crutch.

"We both know why I'm mad. I wasn't given a choice. And today, I made the choice to set this in motion. This." He pointed between the two of us. "Yes, I forced you to marry me. I took your choice away, and maybe that was wrong, but I couldn't figure out a way to balance the feelings I have for you."

"So this was your retribution?"

He shrugged and I wanted to smack him again.

"You married me out of revenge?" My voice rose to a high pitch that I immediately detested.

"No, I married you because I'm in love with you." He pressed his lips together, and his cheeks flared red.

I could almost hear his internal rant for letting that slip.

"But you hate me at the same time," I said, matching his glare.

He shook his head. "That's my problem. No matter how pissed I am at the whole situation, I still want you by my side. I still need you to keep the darkness away. I still fucking love your sweet ass." The words spit out between his clenched teeth.

We stared at each other. His eyes were as wild as I imagined mine were, somewhere between fury and lust, and just being this close to him was clouding some of that aggravation. It was doing the same to him as well. I could feel it in the grip he had on me and the hardness pressing into my pelvic bone.

"Why did you marry me?" he asked.

I laughed and looked at the ceiling. "Beyond your ultimatum?"

He waited while my brain formulated the right words. "Because no matter how mad I am, I still fucking love you, too," I snapped.

"Was there a loophole for you in that spell you cast?"

As much as the question fried my insides, I knew he had to ask. "No. It applied to anyone who stood by your side at the wedding altar." It was my turn to ask a question even though the answer was as dreaded to me as his likely was to him. "Did you know your mother did that to my father?"

He shook his head. "No." He bit his lip like he didn't want to go further with this question and answer session. Like the next question pinging through his mind would undo him if he asked. He forged ahead anyway. "While I was at my trial, did those men..."

The pain in his eyes softened the beast within me, taming it into submission. "No. I got away before they were able to do anything significant beyond whipping me with their belts. The only man I've ever been with, willing or not, is you." I sighed and cupped his cheek.

Relief melted into his muscles as his eyes brimmed with unshed tears.

Now it was my turn. My unwanted question leapt out. "Would you have raped me in that cell if I hadn't head-butted you?"

The tears spilled, rolling down his cheeks as he nodded. His chin trembled when he opened his mouth and forced a "Yes."

"Were you aware of the things you were doing?" I asked. His pain hurt deep, but I needed to know. I hadn't seen any recognition of who I was or what he was doing to me present in his eyes at the time. The blankness had scared the living shit out of me.

His eyes squeezed closed and he nodded. "But no matter how much I tried to gain control, I couldn't until you bashed my nose." He squeezed me tighter and pressed his lips to my temple. "I'm sorry," he whispered and took a breath before meeting my gaze. "Did you cut off my leg to save me?"

"Yes, and I'm not at all sorry for making that choice."

"Have you lost faith in me?" he asked, his voice soft and scared.

"No. I'll never lose faith in you as long as you stay true to who you really are. And I'm not talking about the asshole you portray out there." I pointed to the door. "I'm talking about the man who considered the cosmos with me on the roof, the one who I used to race with, laugh with, and even argue philosophy with. I will never lose faith in you as long as you keep true to that man. You may have hidden that part of yourself from the rest of the sector, but I've seen it. I've seen the kindness in you. I've seen your heart."

He pulled me into his arms, dropping the crutch to the ground. One hand threaded into my hair, and the other pressed into my lower back. His lips greedily covered my mouth while his tongue played with mine, exploring, teasing, toying with the tumult of emotions riding my body.

"Jaden," I whispered under the pressure of him.

I wasn't ready for this. Not with the thundering of my heart and the tightness in my stomach. I knew he wanted to take me to bed and ravish every inch of me, but I needed to clear my head. I needed to let go of all this pain and anger before I could truly be his.

"I can't. Not yet," I said and peeled out of his arms. Before I was aware of what I was doing, I had already fled the hotel room and bounded down the stairs and out into the street. My feet took me where I usually ran. I grabbed my mother's blanket and climbed to the roof.

It wasn't as easy in a wedding dress, but I needed time, space, and a moment before I could move forward.

STAR CROSSED

Chapter 26

I stood with the dress billowing around me and my mother's blanket wrapped around my shoulders. This should have been the happiest day of my life, but it was far from that. Tears bathed my face as I sought comfort in the afghan and the lingering scent of Jaden's cologne.

A scraping sound pulled my attention away from the view, and I glanced over my shoulder. Jaden pulled himself onto the asphalt roofing and rolled onto his back, huffing from exertion. Seeing him lying there covered in a thin sheen of sweat gave me a start.

"What the hell do you think you're doing?" I asked, wiping my face.

"Chasing after my bride who took off like the building was on fire," he said through wheezing breaths. "I didn't realize marrying me was such an emotional fuck up." He pushed himself into a sitting position.

"It's my wedding day," I said as fresh tears spilt hot paths down my cheeks. "I should be happy."

He struggled to his feet, hopped over to the air vent, and used it to come closer to where I stood.

"What are we doing?" I asked him.

"Hell if I know." His green eyes held the Jaden I had known for years, the Jaden I loved with all my heart. "What do you want to be doing?"

"Making love to you in the hotel," I said, cursing the damn truth serum. I pressed my lips together.

"Then what are you doing up here?" His eyes implored me, begging for an answer that made sense.

"Running away from the overwhelming feelings hitting me from every angle." I closed my eyes and hung my head, taking a deep breath before I met his gaze again.

He held his hand out, and I took it, moving into his arms.

"Tell me what's going on in your head?" his soft voice whispered in my ear.

"My parents are dead, and I killed your mother," I whispered as my demons finally caught up with me. Sobs shook my form. "And Gypsy was killed because she helped me."

He kissed my cheek and hooked his finger under my chin, making me look at him.

"And it's my wedding day," I whispered.

"It's okay, Star. You've lost a lot in such a short time. You're allowed to mourn your parents and Gypsy." He brushed my tears away. "And as for my mother, you killed her in self-defense."

"What about you? Aren't you the least bit sad your mother is dead?"

He shook his head. "I was ready to kill her myself, remember? The only deaths I expect to be mourning are my little brother's and your mom's. Those haven't quite hit yet, and I'm sure I'm going to be a fucking mess whenever it finally sinks in." He stroked my hair softly, and his smile faded. "Are we too damaged to get through this?"

I considered his question as he searched my eyes. We were both damaged by all that had happened, but there wasn't anyone else I wanted by my side to help put the pieces back together. He was the only one with the power to fix the heaviness in my heart. I finally shook my head, and he pulled me close, leaning on me for support. He wrapped his arms around me.

"How about we go back where it's warm and have some champagne and wedding cake," he whispered in my ear. "And then make love for the rest of the night."

"You sure you'll have the energy for that? You're barely holding yourself up right now."

He smiled and there he was in full force. The Jaden I loved stood before me, flashing his infamous grin, and that sparkle in his green irises told me more than words could ever say.

"As long as I don't fall to my death from this rooftop, or break my back or something equally as morbid."

"How the hell did you get up here, anyway?" I glanced behind him at the hole and the ropes we used to scale together.

"Raw determination and a little extra boost." He tapped his temple.

I gave him an eye roll and took a moment to scan the horizon.

"In case I forget, you look stunning today," he said.

I turned towards him and gave him a sniffling smile. "You look damn fine in that tuxedo."

"Even without two legs?" He looked away from me. Apprehension drew lines around his mouth, and he licked his lips.

I cocked my head to the side, capturing his attention before I spoke. "Yes. You will never be crippled in my eyes. Challenged, maybe, but a cripple? Never, and I'll never treat you that way."

"So you're not going to carry me down the rope on your back?" The dimple I loved so dearly played in his cheek as he tried not to smile.

"And ruin this dress? You, my friend are out of your mind. Besides, I'm already carrying my mother's blanket down. Unless you wanted to carry it?" I asked, trying to suppress my own smile.

"Aren't you just such a sweet and thoughtful girl," he said with a teasing grin. When he glanced at the opening, his smile faded. "In all seriousness, I am going to need help. I really don't quite know what I was thinking when I climbed up here."

"How do you want to do this?" I asked.

Usually we just hopped on the ropes and slid down by wrapping our legs around the nylon and letting the fabric slide through our loose hands until we reached the stairwell and jumped off. It was all very physical and daunting because of the way we used both feet. I had never climbed down hand over hand, which is what Jaden would have to do.

"I think I might need more help at the bottom, so you go first," he said.

"Why don't we do this at the same time? That way if you get into trouble, I'll be right there to help."

"Is this like the whole 'you die, I die' thing?"

I laughed and shook my head. "No, it's more along the lines of let's do something incredibly stupid together."

"Like get married?"

"Yes. Exactly," I said, and we both broke out in smiles.

"I'm sorry I was such a dick."

I squeezed his hand. "You're allowed to have a bad day every now and then. Just don't make it a habit."

"By the way, I don't think I ever thanked you for that." He nodded towards the boundaries of sector eleven.

Even I had to admit the wall of white flame was beautiful. I silently thanked the elements for helping form such a gorgeous safety feature. It glowed for a moment, acknowledging my thoughts.

"It's almost as beautiful as you are."

Rolling my eyes and uttering a laugh, I led him to the ropes, making sure he had his rope in his hands before I jumped, and grabbed mine while I was airborne.

Jaden's face was a mask of concentration as he dangled from the rope, sliding one hand down before the other. His arms strained against the fabric of the suit, and a thin layer of sweat broke out on his forehead. When we finally made it down the four flights of rubble and reached the landing where his crutches leaned on the far wall, I thought we might just make it without incident.

I climbed over the railing first.

He swung, trying to catch the railing with his leg and missed.

My internal siren started, and I reached out at the very moment he lost his grip on the rope. I caught his wrist, and his frazzled gaze met mine as I slammed into the railing, nearly toppling over with him.

"Gods, give me strength," I uttered and braced myself against the iron, pulling upwards with everything I had. My muscles strained. Every ounce of strength I had rippled and shook.

Jaden's free hand grabbed hold of the railing. I maneuvered his other hand to the bar, making sure he had a grip before I let go and reached for his belt. With Herculean strength, I hauled him over the railing to safety before we both collapsed on the stairs, huffing from exertion.

The way my heart slammed against my ribcage, you would have thought it was trying to make a break for it. I sucked in air, trying to catch my breath as hot blood pumped though me, heating my entire form with an exhilarated tingle.

Jaden gasped as he stared at the hole in the roof. "That really was stupid."

"It certainly provided that adrenaline rush we are both accustomed to," I said.

His rich laughter echoed on the walls and I smiled, staring up at the first signs of nightfall.

STAR CROSSED

Chapter 27

We tumbled onto the bed at the hotel a half hour later. The adrenaline had long since disappeared. Jaden rolled his head lazily towards me.

"I may have exaggerated back there," he said.

Jaden looked every bit as tired as I felt. My muscles quivered with the expense of energy. "You don't have any energy left?"

He shook his head. "Not a lick." Even his voice sounded exhausted.

"Then how about a bubble bath instead? The tub has amazing water jets." I was in need of a shower or something, and another pampering bath sounded like heaven, especially if I shared that oversized tub with Jaden. Maybe that would spark a little energy between us.

His tired smile faded, and worry replaced it as he glanced in the direction of the bathroom.

"What's wrong?"

He opened his mouth to speak, but nothing came out. His sudden panic filled the space between us, and he just shook his head.

"Look at me," I said, and he met my gaze. "What is wrong?"

"I didn't think this through," he said, his voice quiet and full of regret.

"Think what through?" Now I was scared. Did he have doubts about marrying me? My head filled with horrible thoughts as the panic in the air affected me.

"Undressing."

I suddenly understood. His apprehension had nothing to do with me and everything to do with his own insecurity. "I've already seen you naked. So, what gives?"

"I'm worried that my leg will completely turn you off."

I rolled towards him, propped my head up on my hand, and reached for him. I leaned in and gave him a soft kiss. When I pulled away, I said, "You do realize that it's you who turns me on and not your body parts, right?"

That pulled a smile to his lips, but it disappeared as quickly as it came.

"Do you want to take a bath?" I asked, attacking it a different way.

"Yes. I sweated like a pig coming down that rope, and it would be nice to feel clean."

"Okay, then you start the bath, get in, and when you're ready, you let me know and I'll join you," I said. Otherwise I was just going to soak until he built up the nerves to join me.

He considered my offer and then nodded. "I'm not saying that will take away all my angst, but it would help."

"Before you disappear into the bathroom, can you unzip?" I rolled, giving him access to the back of my dress. The click of the zipper slowly going down created a heat inside me. I glanced over my shoulder. "Can you also unclasp the bra?"

He offered up a smile as he reached with his forefinger and thumb and unclasped the bra hook in one quick motion. Then he climbed out of bed and picked up his crutches.

I stared at the ceiling while he filled up the tub. When the jets started, he let out a little chuckle.

I rolled off the bed, letting the dress and bra fall to the ground. "You ready?"

"Yeah, but good luck finding me," he said.

I crossed to the door and laughed at the sight of bubbles reaching three feet higher than the rim of the tub.

"It kind of exploded in bubbles when I turned on the jets." He cleaned out a path, knocking suds over the edge. When he finally cleared enough for me to see him, his goofy smile warmed my soul.

I slid my underwear off and crossed to the edge of the tub. His gaze lingered on my body long enough for me to become self-conscious, but I didn't try to hide myself. If I was going to ease his unrest, he would have to see me accepting all my flaws, too.

I stepped into the hot water, and he guided me between his legs. I settled in the sea of bubbles and turned my head enough to capture a peck before leaning against him. He wrapped his arms around me and kissed my neck, nuzzling and creating a delicious shiver.

We sat in silence, letting the tub create bubbles around us. When I dropped my hands to his thighs, he stiffened and not in the right places. I craned my neck and met his gaze.

"Relax," I whispered, but the tightness in his arms and his thighs didn't abate. I leaned my head back on his shoulder and closed my eyes, trying to take my own advice.

The bubbles receded enough to get glimpses of the water when his lips found the curve of my neck. His arms loosened and his hands started exploring, caressing my breasts before venturing between my legs. He lifted his good leg, snaking it around mine to spread my legs wider.

His fingers slowly circled my clit, and I let out a soft moan of contentment. My hands gripped his thighs as his caress turned insistent. He shifted so he could slide his fingers inside me while he continued to play my clit like a guitar string. Tingling sensations filled me along with a burning need, and my breath quickened. His hardness pressed against my lower back.

"Come for me, Star," he whispered against my neck, his voice husky with need. He rolled the hard nubs of my breasts between his fingers as the hand between my legs created magic.

"Jaden," I whispered, arching my back and turning my head to capture a kiss.

His mouth covered mine, and our tongues mingled in frantic beats. The heat inside me built to a level I had never experienced. I moaned in his mouth as the wave rode through me, curling my toes and clenching my muscles.

He continued to stroke me, creating strong aftershocks. I wanted him inside me. I wanted to feel the pressure of his cock filling every inch of me, not just his fingers.

I broke the kiss, breathless, and stared into his eyes. "I want you. Now."

His hand paused, and he wiggled his fingers inside me, teasing as a smile found his lips. "Right now?" He wiggled them again and brushed his thumb across my sensitive clit.

My body reacted and I sighed. "Yes!"

His hands moved away, and he twisted me towards him until I was in a straddle position. He lined himself up with my aching core and then pulled me down hard.

I gasped and his eyes sparkled. He leaned forward and took my breast in his mouth, sucking and teasing with his teeth. Water sloshed in the tub with our frantic thrusts, creating a mess on the bathroom floor.

This wasn't at all like our first time. It was the exact opposite of that gentle love making session. This was need-ridden and hard, and each plunge pulled a gasp from me and brought me closer to another edge.

"Oh. My. God."

He grabbed my hair and pulled me to his lips. Our tongues matched the pace, and our moans muffled in our mouths. His grip on my hips tightened, as did every muscle in both our bodies. I pulled away from his mouth, arching with the strength of the orgasm.

As soon as the aftershocks faded, I collapsed into his arms. His chest heaved just as much as mine.

"Holy shit," he whispered against my neck. He sprawled his arms over the edge of the tub, leaned his head back against the rim, and closed his eyes.

"No kidding." I circled my hips, just to make a point, and he smiled but didn't move. "Are you ready for some of that cake?"

One eye opened, and dimples appeared in his cheeks. "I could eat some cake. Why don't you get out and grab a couple of towels or something."

I shifted, suddenly ravenous, and we both winced from the uncoupling. I climbed out of the tub and grabbed an oversize towel, wrapping it around my body before I handed one to Jaden. He was still sitting in the tub, his cheeks red.

"Just throw it over the crutch, and I'll be out in a minute," he said.

I gave him a nod and left.

He came out a few minutes later with the towel wrapped tightly around his waist. It reached below the knee, hiding the end of his leg. He crossed to where I stood, next to the cake and champagne. The color remained in his cheeks, and he avoided looking directly at me.

"Jaden?"

His gaze flitted to mine and then away. "Want some champagne with your cake?" He pointed with his chin.

"Sure."

He closed the distance and uncorked the champagne with ease before pouring two glasses. Handing me one, he finally met my gaze.

"I'm not sure what to toast to," he said.

"To a long and healthy marriage?" I raised my glass. "To a much smoother relationship than what we started with?"

He let out a soft laugh. "How about to a marriage filled with fire and adrenaline."

"And laughter," I added, tapping my glass to his.

"And laughter," he said, doing the same.

We both drained our glasses and turned towards the cake. Instead of waiting for him to cut a piece, I swiped my finger across the frosting and brought it to his lips. His eyebrow rose, but he opened his mouth and let me slip my finger inside.

Jaden sucked the frosting off while he wiped a finger full of frosting and brought it to my lips. I sucked it off slowly, twirling my tongue around his finger. He let out a low growl that turned on the wild switch inside me.

When he pulled his finger from my mouth, I purred, "Is there something else you'd like me to suck?"

He chuckled and I grabbed the front of his towel, pulling him closer and planting a hungry kiss. My energy levels spiked, and I unraveled his towel before he could stop me. He stiffened under my lips. I dipped two fingers into the frosting before stepping away and swirling the sweet confection on his already hard member.

I had him at a disadvantage, one I knew he wasn't comfortable with, but I lowered to my knees. Before he could react, I slipped the tip of his frosting covered cock in my mouth. His breath caught in his throat, and the knuckles on his hand holding the crutch turned white, but he didn't stop me.

Considering this was my first time ever sucking a man, the bliss on his face told me I wasn't doing a bad job of it at all. I opened my mouth wide and nearly swallowed his full length before sliding my lips down his shaft to his sensitive tip, sucking at the same time. He groaned and threaded his free hand into my hair, guiding me farther up, until his entire length choked me. The force of his hand abated, but his hips rocked with my motion until we matched speed.

His breathing quickened. "Oh, fuck," he groaned as hot cum spurted into my mouth in a shocking wave.

I started to pull away, but his hand kept me in place as the salty semen filled my mouth until I was forced to swallow. He groaned in response, and I sucked until there was nothing left.

His grip loosened, and I sat back on my heels, wiping my mouth with the back of my hand. I took him in, from his satiated gaze down to his heaving chest to his trembling leg still holding him up, all the way down to where I chopped his limb off. The skin was pale and stretched and the stitches had dissolved, but the angry scar still traversed where he'd been sewn together. I reached out, touching his thigh right above his knee, and looked back up at him.

"I love you," I said. "All of you."

It was as if those words were the right elixir, because he pulled me to my feet and kissed me like I was the sexiest woman on earth. He maneuvered us to the bed and climbed on top of me. When the kiss broke, the fire in his eyes left me as breathless as his touch.

He crawled down my body, kissing, nipping, caressing until he settled between my legs. His tongue erased all thought from my brain, and I melted into the sensations. He kept flicking my clit over and over until I panted, and my own juices trickled down the backs of my thighs and ass.

When he finally pulled away, he said, "Hands and knees," while rolling me over.

I obeyed and he was there, filling me with such force I let out a gasp and a groan and nearly collapsed onto my elbows. He grabbed my hips and pounded, hard, filling me with such bravado, I wondered if I'd be able to walk in the morning. That thought vanished as he hit my g-spot and I came harder than I thought possible.

"Holy fuck!" I screamed as it tore through every cell, clenching every muscle. I fell onto my elbows, burying my face into the pillow to drown out the rest of my moan.

Jaden's moans weren't any quieter, and I started to giggle. He collapsed on top of me out of breath, his entire form trembling. I stretched out under him, and he kissed my neck.

"Why are you laughing?" he asked.

"Because between the two of us, we could wake the dead," I said, turning my face away from the pillow.

He started chuckling in my ear. "You are probably right. It's a good thing we are on the top floor. Otherwise they would have called for the authorities already."

My laugh turned into an all out guffaw, and I shook with it. I wasn't the only one laughing, either. Jaden rolled with me so we were tucked together spooning and still coupled, his arms wrapped around me as he laughed into my ear.

"I guess you found some energy reserves." I chuckled and turned my head so I could see him. Unfortunately, my motion forced him out, and we both whined in unison.

"Yeah," he said as his laughter faded into a yawn. "But now I'm truly spent."

My energy levels were tapped as well, and the idea of falling asleep in his arms was dreamlike.

"I'm afraid to go to sleep," I whispered, even though the sandman was knocking on my door in a furious attempt to pull me under.

Jaden shifted and propped himself up on his elbow. "Why?"

I rolled onto my back and palmed his cheek. "Because if this is a dream, I don't want to wake up."

"Go to sleep. I promise you will wake in my arms, and we can eat our breakfast in bed tomorrow and every day after, if that's what you want."

"It's all I've ever wanted."

He leaned over and pressed his lips to mine before settling back into the disheveled sheets with me in his arms. Just before I slipped into slumber, he whispered, "I love you, Star."

I smiled and mumbled 'love you' back before I fell asleep, dreaming of a future where Jaden and I chased after a houseful of children.

THE END

* * *

Thank you for reading Star Crossed. If you enjoyed this book, please consider leaving a review.

About J.E. Taylor

J.E. Taylor is a USA Today bestselling author, a publisher, an editor, a manuscript formatter, a mother, a wife, a business analyst, and a Supernatural fangirl, not necessarily in that order. She first sat down to seriously write in February of 2007 after her daughter asked:

"Mom, if you could do anything, what would you do?"

From that moment on, she hasn't looked back.
In addition to being co-owner of Novel Concept Publishing, Ms. Taylor also moonlights as a Senior Editor of Allegory E-zine, an online venue for Science Fiction, Fantasy and Horror, and co-host of the popular YouTube talk show Spilling Ink.

She lives in Connecticut with her husband and two children and during the summer months enjoys her weekends on the shore in southern Maine.
Visit her at www.jetaylor75.com to check out her other titles.

Sign up for her newsletter on her website for early previews of her upcoming books, release announcements, and special opportunities for free swag!

You might also enjoy her Fractured Fairy Tale series. Find it on her website at www.JETaylor75.com along with other Paranormal Romance and Urban Fantasy stories!